Geoffrey Chaucer

The Knightes Tale

from the Canterbury tales of Geoffrey Chaucer

Geoffrey Chaucer

The Knightes Tale
from the Canterbury tales of Geoffrey Chaucer

ISBN/EAN: 9783337090029

Printed in Europe, USA, Canada, Australia, Japan

Cover: Foto ©Andreas Hilbeck / pixelio.de

More available books at **www.hansebooks.com**

THE KNIGHTES TALE,

FROM

THE CANTERBURY TALES

OF

GEOFFREY CHAUCER.

FROM EDITION OF

REV. RICHARD MORRIS, LL.D.

WITH LIFE, GRAMMAR, NOTES, AND AN ETYMOLOGICAL GLOSSARY.

(*SELECTED.*)

NEW YORK:

CLARK & MAYNARD, PUBLISHERS,

771 BROADWAY AND 67 & 69 NINTH STREET.

A COMPLETE COURSE IN THE STUDY OF ENGLISH.

Spelling, Language, Grammar, Composition, Literature.

Reed's Word Lessons—A Complete Speller.
Reed & Kellogg's Graded Lessons in English.
Reed & Kellogg's Higher Lessons in English.
Kellogg's Text-Book on Rhetoric.
Kellogg's Text-Book on English Literature.

In the preparation of this series the authors have had one object clearly in view—to so develop the study of the English language as to present a complete, progressive course, from the Spelling-Book to the study of English Literature. The troublesome contradictions which arise in using books arranged by different authors on these subjects, and which require much time for explanation in the school-room, will be avoided by the use of the above "Complete Course."

Teachers are earnestly invited to examine these books.

CLARK & MAYNARD, Publishers,
771 Broadway, New York.

LIFE OF CHAUCER.

THE father and grandfather of Geoffrey Chaucer were well-to-do
itizens and vintners of the city of London. The guilds and city
>mpanies were at that time what their names imply, associations of
men engaged in the same trade or industry, and, accordingly, we find
John Chaucer, the father of the poet, keeping a wine-shop and
hostelrie on the banks of the Thames, near the outfall of the Wall
Brook, probably where the Cannon Street Station now stands, and
here Geoffrey was born and spent his early years.

What education he gave his son, and whether he intended him
for the professions of the law or the church, or for the less ambitious
career of a citizen, we do not know.

The author of the " Court of Love" represents himself as " of
Cambridge, clerk;" but even if this could be proved to mean that
he was a student of that university, there are very strong grounds
for believing that the poem has been wrongly attributed to Chaucer.
There is, in fact, not a shadow of evidence that Chaucer studied at
either Oxford or Cambridge, though Leland asserts that he had been
at each.

Young men designed for secular callings frequently finished their
education by attaching themselves to the households or retinue of
some nobleman, with whom they enjoyed the advantages of introduction to good society, and sometimes of foreign travel on political
or military enterprises.

John Chaucer attended Edward III. and his Queen Philippa in
1338 in their expedition to Flanders, but in what capacity we have
no means of learning. In 1357 we find a Geoffrey Chaucer in the
household of Elizabeth, wife of Lionel, third son of Edward, and if
he were our poet he doubtless owed his appointment to his father's
former connection with the court. In 1359 he served, still probably in attendance on Lionel, with the army of Edward in France,
and was, as he himself informs us, taken prisoner, but ransomed in
the following year at the ignominious peace of Bretigny.

In 1367 and the following years we find entries in the Issue Rolls
of the Court of Exchequer and in the Tower Rolls of the payment
to him of a pension of twenty marks for former and present services

as one of the valets of the king's chamber. While in attendance on the members of the royal family he had formed an unreturned and hopeless attachment to some lady of far higher social rank, which inspired his first original poem, the "Compleynt to Pite;" and since, in his elegy on the death of Blanche, the young wife of John of Gaunt, entitled "The Dethe of Blaunche the Duchesse," he confesses that the "sickeness" that he "had suffred this eight yeere" is now past, there can be little doubt that she was the object of his affection.

From 1370 to 1380 he was engaged in not less than seven diplo matic missions to Italy, France, and Flanders, for which he received various sums of money, as well as a valuable appointment in the customs; in 1374 he obtained the lease of the house above the Aldgate from the corporation of London, and in this year the Duke of Lancaster granted him a pension of £10 for services rendered by himself and his wife Philippa. We hear of a Philippp Chaucer as one of the Ladies of the Bedchamber to the Queen Philippa as early as 1366; but since in the "Compleynte to Pite " in 1367 he expresses a hope that his high-born lady love may yet accept his love, it is probable that she was a namesake or cousin of Geoffrey, and that he did not marry her until the nuptials of the Lady Blanche with the duke had extinguished his hopes of ever making her his wife, perhaps, indeed, not until after her death.

In 1372-73 he remained in Italy for nearly a year on the king's business, where, if he did not make the acquaintance of Petrarch and Boccaccio, as is supposed by some, it is certain that the study of the Italian poetry and literature exerted a marked influence on his own writings, as seen in the works composed during this middle period of his literary career, the " Lyfe of Seynte Cecile," " Parlament of Foules," " Compleynt of Mars," "Anelide and Arcite," " Boece," " Former Age," " Troylus and Cresseide," and the " House of Fame."

At a later period he wrote his " Truth," " Legende of Good Women," his " Moder of God," and began the " Canterbury Tales."

In 1386 he was elected a knight of the shire for the county of Kent, and in this year we obtain the only authentic evidence of his age. In a deposition made by him at Westminster, where the parliament was met, in the famous trial between Richard, Lord Scrope, and Sir Robert Grosvenor, the council clerk entered him, doubtless on his own statement, as forty years old and upwards, and as having borne arms for twenty-seven years. We may therefore conclude that he was born in 1339, which would make him at that time forty-seven years old, and the twenty-seven years would count from his coming of age. He would thus have been eighteen when he became page to the Princess Elizabeth, and twenty in the French war.

His patron, John of Gaunt, was now abroad, and John's rival, the Duke of Gloucester, in power. The commission appointed by the parliament to inquire into the administration of the customs and subsidies, dismissed him from his two appointments in the customs, and soon after even his pensions were revoked. He was thus reduced from affluence to poverty, and his feelings are expressed in his beautiful "Balade of Truth;" to add to his troubles his wife died next year (1389), yet amid grief and penury he went on with his merry "Canterbury Tales."

With the reassumption of the government by Richard II. in 1389 and the return of the Lancastrian party to power, fortune smiled once more on the poor poet, but his income was at best small and uncertain, and his tenure of some petty offices short and precarious. He wrote about this time his translation of a "Treatise on the Astrolabe, for his son Lewis," his "Compleynt of Venus," "Envoy to Skogan," "Marriage," "Gentleness," "Lack of Steadfastness," "Fortune and his Compleynt to his Purse," besides carrying on his greatest work, the "Tales," which was left unfinished at his death. This event occurred in 1400 at a house in the garden of the Chapel of St. Mary, Westminster, the lease of which he had taken in the previous year.

He was probably in his sixty-first or sixty-second year when he died.

In the carefully executed portrait by Occleve, preserved among the Harl. MSS., and the words which he puts into the mouth of "mine host" of the Tabard, as well as from admissions no less than deliberate expressions of feeling scattered through his works, we can form a pretty complete notion of his personal appearance, habits, and character.

Stout in body but small and fair of face, shy and reserved with strangers, but fond—perhaps too fond—of "good felaweschip," of wine and song; passionately given to study, often after his day's labours at the customs sitting up half the night poring over old musty MSS., French, Latin, Italian, or English, till his head ached, and his eyes were dull and dazed. But his love of nature was as strong as his love of books. He is fond of dwelling on the beauties of the spring-time in the country.

> " Herkneth these blisful briddēs how they synge,
> And seth the fressché flourēs how they springe!"

he bids us on a bright April morn. And more fully describes his own feelings in the "Legend of Good Women."

> " And as for me, though that I konne but lyte,
> On bokēs for to rede I me delyte,
> And to hem give I feyth and ful credencē,
> And in myn herte have hem in reverencē
> So hertēly that there is gamē noon
> That fro my bokēs maketh me to goon,
> But yt be seldom on the holy day,
> ' Save certeynly whan that the monethe of May
> Is comen, and that I here the foulēs synge,
> And that the flourēs gynnen for to sprynge,
> Faire wel my boke, and my devocioun!"

He was thoroughly English, one of the educated middle class, the class to which England owes so much; he had by his connection with court acquired the refinement and culture of the best French and Italian society, without rising above or severing himself from the people to whom he belonged. He could appreciate genuine worth in squire or ploughman, purity and courtesy whether in knight or in the poor country parson. All were his fellowmen, and he sympathized with all. He had known every change of fortune, of wealth and want, and his poetry often reflects his state for the time being; but even in his old age, when poor, infirm, and alone, his irrepressible buoyancy of spirts did not desert him.

Freshness and simplicity cf style, roguish humour, quaint fun. hearty praise of what is good and true, kindly ridicule of weakness and foibles, and earnest denunciation of injustice and öppression, are among his most marked characteristics.

ESSAY ON THE LANGUAGE OF CHAUCER.

The age of Chaucer marks an epoch in the history of our language, when what is called the New English arose from the complete fusion of the Norman French with the speech of the common people.

So long as our kings retained their continental possessions, and our nobles ruled England as a conquered country, looking to Normandy, Picardy, and Anjou as their fatherland, whence they continually recruited their numbers, the union of the races was impossible; but with the final loss of Normandy by King John in 1204 the relations of the two countries were changed, and in the reign of Edward I. and Edward III. the Norman barons were compelled by circumstances to consider this their home, and France a land to be reconquered by the arms of their English fellow-citizens and subjects. The change of sentiment required, however, time for its completion. For two or three generations the nobles felt themselves a superior race and clung to their own language, disdaining to adopt one which they had been accustomed to look on as fit only for "villans and burghers." Though they could not abstain from intercourse with the common people, the separation of language persisted, and served to mark the man of rank from the plebeian.

In the metrical chronicle of Robert of Gloucester, which from internal evidence must have been written later than A.D. 1280, and is referred by Mr. K. Oliphant to about A.D. 1300, it is plainly asserted, that to speak French was in his time considered a mark of good breeding:

> " Vor bote a man couthe French me tolth of hym wel lute,
> Ac lowe men holdeth to Engliss, and to her owe speche yute;
> Ich wene ther ne be man in world contreyes none
> That ne holdeth to her kunde speche bote Engelond one;
> Ac wel me wot vor to conne bothe wel yt ys,
> Vor the more that a man can the more worthe he is."

> [For unless a man know French one thinks but little of him,
> But low men hold to English, and to their own speech well;

9

I believe there are no men in the countries of the world
That do not hold to their native speech but England only;
But well I know that it is well to understand both,
For the more that a man knows the more worth (able) he is.]

The blending of the languages began with the fourteenth century. The ballads of Lawrence Minot, composed probably at intervals between 1330 and 1360, and the " Vision of Piers Plowman," which seems to have been written soon after 1365, contain an infusion of French words; but the effects of the complete coalescence of the two peoples, and the impulse it gave to the development of the common language, are to be seen in the poems of Gower and his friend Chaucer, which belong to the latter part of the fourteenth century. The translation of the Bible into English by Wycliffe at the same time served to raise the literary character and to fix the grammatical forms of the language, which had been passing through a period of rapid changes.

The old system of inflexions had been undergoing a process of disintegration, the several endings in *e*, *a*, *en*, and *an*, by which cases and numbers, moods and adverbs, had hitherto been distinguished, were fast being for the most part replaced by the single form of *e*, partly as a result of a law in every language that words become worn down by use, like pebbles in a water-course smoothed and rounded by friction,—a change which proceeds most rapidly in the absence of a written literature, and tends to convert synthetic or inflected into analytic or uninflected languages; and partly in obedience to a law less general, only because its conditions are not universal, viz. that when two races speaking different languages are merged into one, they, though freely using one another's words, being unable to agree as to their inflections, end by discarding such syllables altogether so far as can be done without loss of perspicuity.

To this law may be referred the triumph of the plural sign *s* or *es* over *en* or *an*, since French and English found themselves here at least at one, and the same may be said of the prefixes *un* and *in*, and the suffixes *able* and *ible*.

This detrition of inflexions, as we may call it, culminated in the Elizabethan era in the almost total loss of the final *e*, before the expedients for distinguishing infinitives from participles, adverbs from adjectives, &c., had been reduced to rule. Its loss becomes a stumbling-block to readers of Shakespeare and his contemporaries scarcely less grievous than its retention does to those of Chaucer, appearing in the guise of inexplicable anomalies, and of seeming violations of the most ordinary grammatical rules, which have been laboriously cleared up by Dr. Abbott in his admirable *Shakespearian Grammar*.

But though the new English had fairly established itself as a national and literary language it was still in a state of rapid growth and development, destined to undergo considerable changes in grammar, and even more in orthography, ere it settled down into the form which it has retained without any material alteration from the time of the Stuarts to the present day.

When Chaucer wrote printing was not yet invented; a number of scribes, whose attainments did not perhaps go beyond the mere mechanical art of writing, were accustomed to work together while one read aloud the book to be copied, and each spelling as he was in the habit of pronouncing, and probably not seldom misapprehending the meaning of the author, it was inevitable that countless variations should arise in the text, some representing the sound of the spoken word, others the changes which had taken place in the pronunciation between the dates of the original MS. and the particular copy, and others still such clerical blunders as are even now familiar to every one who has had to correct the proofs of any literary work.

After the sixteenth century, when our language had become stereotyped as it were in grammar and orthography, various attempts were made to modernize the spelling of so popular a poet as Chaucer so as to make him intelligible to ordinary readers, but with the most unhappy results; the men who undertook the task being almost entirely ignorant of the essential features of the language of the original work.

With a prose writer the consequences might not have been more serious than the loss to posterity of an invaluable philological landmark; but where metre and rime were involved, the result has been the entire destruction of all that constitutes the outward form of poetry; while by the subsequent attempts of editors to restore to the mangled verses something like metrical rhythm, the language itself has been wrested and corrupted to an extent which would have rendered hopeless all idea of its restoration, were it not that in the Harleian MS. 7334 we possess a copy executed by a competent hand very shortly after the author's death, and though not free from clerical errors, on the whole remarkably correct. The late learned antiquary Mr. Thomas Wright adopted it in his edition, with a few emendations; but since the publication by Mr. F. T. Furnivall of his six-text edition of Chaucer we have the means of collating it with the Ellesmere, Hengwrt, Corpus, Lansdowne, Petworth, and Cambridge MSS. Dr. Morris has availed himself of the first three in his edition of the "Prologue, the Knightes and the Nonnes Tales" (Clarendon Press Series); but though he has consulted the last three also in cases of difficulty, he has found them of little real use.

Chaucer himself seems to have had forebodings of the mutilations which were to befall his works, having already suffered from the negligence of his amanuensis. for in the closing stanzas of his "Troilus and Cressida," he says,

> " Go litel booke, go litel tragedie,
> And for ther is so grete diversitè
> In Englisch and in writing of our tong.
> So pray I God that non miswritè thee,
> Ne thee mismetre for defaut of tong.
> And rede wherso thou be or eles song
> That thou be understond."

And in language more forcible than elegant he imprecates a curse on this unlucky man—

> " Adam Scrivener, if evere it thee bifal
> Boece or Troilus for to writè new,
> Under thy long lokkes maist thou have the scall,
> But after my making thou write more trew.
> So ofte a day I mote thy werke renew,
> It to correct and eke to rubbe and scrape,
> And al is thorow thy negligence and rape."

HISTORY OF THE ENGLISH LANGUAGE TO THE TIME OF CHAUCER.

The term Anglo-Saxon, which is currently used to designate the language supposed to have been spoken by our forefathers before the Norman Conquest, is an invention of modern times, and has not even the advantage of convenience to recommend it.

It was not until the close of the thirteenth and beginning of the fourteenth century, when the fusion of races was followed by the rise of a truly national spirit and an outburst of literary activity, that a national language had any existence. The greater part of the thirteenth century was a period of dearth and degradation, a dark age to the student and lover of our glorious tongue. What little was written was in Latin or French, English being considered not only by the proud nobles, but unhappily also by a pedantic priesthood, as unworthy of cultivation, and consequently, being relegated to the ignorant peasantry, it suffered the loss of thousands of good old words. Hitherto the clergy had written in the language of the people to whom they belonged, and had produced many works of great literary merit. These, however, may be easily recognized as belonging to two great dialectic divisions—a north-eastern and south-western, besides minor subdivisions. The great sundering line may roughly be drawn from Shrewsbury through Northampton and Bedford to Colchester, and represents the original partition of the country between the Angles and the Saxons. On the former fell the full force of the Danish invasions, and as we go further north we find the proportion of Scandinavian words and forms to increase.

In the earliest times these languages were almost as distinct as High German and Low German (Platt Deutsch), and the so-called Anglo-Saxon dictionaries confound and mingle the two without distinction. The infusion of Danish or Norse into the Anglian led naturally to a clipping and paring down of inflections, a feature common to all mixed languages; whereas the speech of Wessex, the kingdom of Alfred, preserved much longer its rich inflectional character. Yet even these south-western people seem to have called themselves English rather than Saxons. At any rate King Alfred tells us that his people called their speech English, and Robert of Gloucester says of English, "The Saxones speche yt was, and thorw hem ycome yt ys." Bede, an Angle, calls them Saxons, but the word is of rare occurrence before the thirteenth century. Procopius in the sixth century calls them Frisians.

It is, however, from the East Midland chiefly that the new English arose, where the monks of Peterborough compiled the history of England in English, in chronicles which were copied and scattered throughout the land. Their dialect incorporating all that was good from the others laid the foundation of that literary language which, again taking up a large French element, was destined to become the speech of the nation at large.

Early in the fourteenth century Robert of Brunne, called also Robert Manning, living in Rutland, in the same linguistic province as the monks of Peterborough, wrote *The Handlyng Synne*, which marks an era in the history of our language and literature. In it may be seen actually or foreshadowed every feature of language, idiom, and grammar which distinguishes the English of to-day from that of King Alfred and from the Teutonic languages of the Continent. His English is no longer inflectional but analytic, the difference being one of kind not of degree merely, as was the case in the Old Anglian when compared with the speech of the West Saxons. Of the language of *The Handlyng Synne* we may say as Sir Philip Sidney did of the Elizabethan age, " English is void of those cumbersome differences of cases, genders, moods, and tenses, which I think was a piece of the Tower of Babylon's curse, that a man should be put to schoole to learne his mother tongue; but for the uttering sweetly and properly the conceit of the minde, which is the ende of speech, that it hath equally with any other tongue in the world."

Of scarcely less value as marking another feature of our present language is the *Ancren Riwle*, written about 1220 by a learned prelate, into which French and Latin words are imported wholesale. Chaucer has been accused of corrupting our language; but if we compare his works with the *Ancren Riwle*, written a century and a half earlier, we shall find that the affectation of French words and idioms by the author of the *Riwle*, an example which for nearly a hundred years none had dared to follow, puts Chaucer rather in the light of a restorer of our language, and justifies Spenser's description of him as "a well of English undefiled." He did not affect a retrograde course, but endeavoured to develop the new powers which English had acquired from this "happy marriage," the fruit of which has been described by none in more glowing terms than by the profound German scholar Grimm. " None of the modern languages has through the very loss and decay of all phonetic laws, and through the dropping of nearly all inflections, acquired greater force and vigour than the English, and from the fulness of those vague and indefinite sounds which may be learned but can never be taught, it has derived a power of expression such as has never been at the command of any human tongue. Begotten by a surprising union of the two noblest languages of Europe, the one Teutonic, the other Romanic, it received that wonderfully happy temper and thorough breeding, where the Teutonic supplied the material strength, the Romanic the suppleness and freedom of expression. . . . In wealth, in wisdom, and strict economy, none of the living languages can vie with it." Such being the character of the language in which Chaucer wrote, it is not necessary to give in detail the grammatical forms and inflections of the older English dialects.

It will be sufficient to indicate such as were still in use, but have been subsequently dropped or so worn down as to be no longer easily recognized, and to show at the same time how these are modified by the necessities of metrical composition, so as to be lost to the ear though properly retained in the orthography, in accordance with rules of prosody not unlike those familiar to readers of Latin and French poetry, and which held their ground more or less in English down to the time of Milton.

The use of the final *e* in the language of the fourteenth and fifteenth centuries presents the greatest difficulty to all who are unacquainted with the grammatical construction of the early and middle English. It was not, as it now is, a merely conventional sign for marking the long sound of the preceding vowel, as in the modern words *băr* and *bāre*, for which purpose it is indifferent whether it is placed at the end of the syllable or immediately before the vowel to be lengthened, as in *bāre* or *beār*, *sēre* or *seēr;* nor was it, as in the sixteenth and seventeenth centuries, inserted or omitted at the whim of the writer or convenience of the printer, when we may often see the same word spelled with and without it in the same or consecutive lines; nor was it, as in the artificial would-be antiquated diction of Spenser's *Faerie Queene*, employed without any certain rule either as "an aping of the ancients," as Ben Jonson called it, or for lengthening out the line to the number of syllables required by the peculiar metre borrowed from the Italian poets, and to which the more rigid English tongue would otherwise have refused to bend; but it was a real grammatical inflection, marking case and number, distinguishing adverbs from the corresponding adjectives, and in certain verbs of the "strong" form representing the -*en* of the older plural, *e.g.* he *spak, thei spake,* for *spaken*, like the German *er sprach, sie sprachen;* so that to write, as the modernized texts havĕ it, *he spake,* would be a blunder as gross as the converse *they speaks* would be now, and to pronounce *they spake* as we do is to rob the line of a syllable and the verse of its rhythm and metre, and, if the word be at the end, it may be of its rime, as for instance where the indirect objective cases *timé* and *Romé* rime with *by me* and *to me.*

The following summary of the peculiar features of Chaucer's grammar is founded on the essay of Prof. Child, and Dr. Morris' Introduction to his Chaucer's Prologue, &c., mentioned above.

NOUNS.

NUMBER.—1. The plural is mostly formed by adding -ĕs, pronounced as a distinct syllable.

> " And with his stremĕs dryeth in the grevĕs
> The silver dropĕs hongyng on the levĕs."
> Knightes Tale, ll. 637–8.

-s, which has now almost entirely replaced the -ĕs, was as a rule
used only in words of more than one syllable and in those ending
with a liquid, as *palmers, pilgrims, naciouns*, &c.

Such forms as *bestis, othus*, are probably the provincial or dialecti-
cal usages of the scribes employed.

2. Some nouns form their plurals in -*en* or -*n* (the -*an* of O.E.), as
asschen, been (bees), *eyghen* (eyes) [Scot. *een*], *flon* (arrows), *schoon*
(shoes), [Scot. *shoon*], and *oxen; fon* or *foon* (foes), and *kyn*, which
remained till the seventeenth century as *kine*.

3. *Brethren, children*, with the obsolete *doughtren* and *sistren*, are
formed by adding -*n* to an older plural form in O.E. -*e*, A.S. -*u*.
The O.E. *childre*, &c., persists as *childer*, &c., in the provincial dialect
of the northern counties.

4. *Deer, scheep, swin* have never had a plural termination; *folk*,
hors, night, thing, and *yeer* or *yer* have acquired such only in recent
times, the plural in the earlier ages of our language having had the
same form as the singular.

5. *Feet, men, geese, teeth* are plurals formed by a vowel change
only.

CASE.—1. The possessive case singular is formed by adding -ĕs
(now mostly -*s*).

> " Ful worthi was he in his lordĕs werre."   Prol. l. 47.

2. The possessive plural had the same form, *foxĕs* tales, *mennĕs*
wittes. But when the nominative ended in -*en* it was sometimes
unchanged, as " his *eyghen* sight."

3. In O.E. *fader, brother, doughter* were uninflected in the possessive case; thus " my *fader* soule," Prol. 781; " *brother* sone,"
K. T. 2226.

4. Some old feminines of the Saxon 1st declension, which made
their possessives in -*an*, had dropped the termination; thus we find
ladyĕ grace, *sonnĕ* upriste (rising), *hertĕ* blood, *widewĕ* sone, and we
still speak of *Lady* day and *Lady* bird.

5. The indirect objective (dative) occurs sometimes as a distinct
case, and ends in -*ĕ*, as *holtĕ, beddĕ*, &c,

ADJECTIVES

Now uninflected had in early English two forms, the definite and indefinite, the former used after demonstrative adjectives, of which the so-called definite article is one, and possessive pronouns (thus differing from the modern German usage), and the indefinite in all other circumstances. In Saxon each was declined, but in Chaucer the only inflection is found in the definite form which ends in -ĕ, as "the yongĕ sonne," "his halfĕ cours." This -ĕ is however generally dropped in words of more than one syllable.

The vocative case of adjectives is distinguished by an -e, as "leevĕ brother," K. T. 326, "O strongĕ God," except in words of French origin, and therefore of recent introduction, as "gentil sire."

DEGREES OF COMPARISON.—The comparative is generally formed as now by adding -er to the positive. The O.E. termination was -re, which is retained in derre (dearer), ferre (farther), nerre (nearer), sorre (sorer).

Lenger, strenger, and the extant elder are examples of inflection together with vowel change.

Bet (bettre or better) and mo (for more) are contracted forms.

The superlative is made by adding -este or -est to adjectives and -est to adverbs; hext (highest), and next, extant (nighest), are contractions.

The plural is formed by adding -ĕ, not -es, "smalĕ fowlĕs," Prol. 9; but adjectives of more than one syllable, and all when used predicatively, drop the -e. Some French words form the plural in -es, as "places delitables."

DEMONSTRATIVES.

In O.E. the so-called definite article the was in the plural tho, a form occasionally, though very rarely, used by Chaucer. The neuter singular was that, but except in the phrases "that oon" and "that other," contracted into toon and tother, Chaucer never uses that otherwise than as we do now.

He frequently employs tho for those, as "tho wordĕs," and "oon of tho that," and he writes the plural of this as thise, thes, or these indiscriminately.

Attĕ, a word of very frequent occurrence, is a corruption of the Saxon at tham, the old objective, O.E. attan, atta, masc. and neut., atter, fem., "attĕ beste," "attĕ Bow,"

Thilkĕ = the like (A.S. *thyllic, thylc*), "*thilkĕ* text," Prol. 182, = that text. *Swich*, Prol. 3, and *sikĕ*, Prol. 245 (A.S. *swylk* = *swa lyk*) = *so like*, our *such*.

That ilke = the same (A.S. *ilk*). Scotch, "Graham of that *ilk*," *i.e.* of that same clan or place [must not be confounded with the Scotch *ilka*, A.S. *ælc* = each]. *Same* did not come into use till about the year 1200.

Som . . . som = one . . . another.

> " He moot ben deed, the kyng as schal a page;
> *Som* in his bed, *som* in the deepĕ see,
> *Som* in the largĕ feeld, as men may se."
> Knightes Tale, 2172-4.

PRONOUNS.

SINGULAR.		PLURAL.
Nom.	I, Ich, Ik,	we.
Poss.	min (myn), mi (my),	our, oure.
Obj.	me,	us.
Nom.	thou (thow),	ye.
Poss.	thin (thyn), thi (thy),	your, youre.
Obj.	the, thee.	yow, you.

	Masc.	Fem.	Neut.	All Genders.
Nom.	he,	she,	hit, it, yt,	thei, they.
Poss.	his,	hire, hir,	his,	here, her, hir.
Obj.	him,	hire, hir, here,	hit, it, yt,	hem.

Independent or predicative forms are *min* (pl. *mine*); *oure, oures; thin* (pl. *thine*); *youre, youres; hire, heres* (hers); *here, heres* (theirs). The forms *owres* and *youres* were borrowed from the Northern dialect.

Thou is often joined to its verb, as *schaltow, woldestow,* Nonne Prestes Tale, 525; *crydestow,* Knightes Tale, 225.

The objective (dative) cases of pronouns are used after impersonal verbs, as "*me* mette;" "*him* thoughte;" after some verbs of motion, as "goth *him;*" "he rydeth *him;*" and after such words as *wel, wo, loth,* and *leef.*

Whos (*whose*) and *whom* are the possessive and objective cases of *who.*

Which is joined with *that,* thus, "Hem *whiche that* wepith;" "His love *the which that* he oweth." Alone it sometimes stands for what or what sort of, as—

> " *Which a* miracle ther befel anoon."
>> Knightes Tale, 1817.
> " And *whiche* they weren, and *of what* degre."
>> Prol. 40.

What is used for *why* like the Lat. *quid*,

> " *What* schulde he studie and make himselven wood?"
>> Prol. 184.

That is sometimes used with a personal pronoun along with it, thus—

> " A knight ther was, and that a worthi man,
> *That* from the tymĕ that he first began
> To ryden out, *he* lovede chivalrye."
>> Prol. 43–45.

> "Al were they sorĕ hurt, and namely oon,
> *That* with a spere was thirled *his* brest boon."
>> Knightes Tale, 1851–2.

In the second instance, *that his* = whose.

Who and *who so* are used indefinitely in the same way as our "*one* says," "As *who* seith," " *Who so* that can him rede," Prol. 741.

Men and the shortened form *me*, which must not be confounded with the objective of *I*, were used from a very early period down to the seventeenth century in the sense of " one," like the German "*man* sagt," &c., and the French "*on* dit," &c. "Me *tolth*" in the passage quoted from Robert of Gloucester (see page 15) is an instance, and one of the latest is to be found in Lodge's *Wits Miserie.*

> " And stop *me* (let *one* stop) his dice, you are a villaine."

VERBS.

I. The so-called weak verbs, or those which form the past tense by the addition of the suffix *-ed*, were thus declined:—

Present Tense.

SINGULAR.	PLURAL.
1. I lovĕ,	We lov-en or lovĕ.
2. Thou lov-est,	Ye lov-en or lovĕ.
3. He lov-eth,	They lov-en or lovĕ.

Past Tense.

1. I lov-ede,	We lov-eden, lov-ede.
2. Thou lov-edest,	You lov-eden, lov-ede.
3. He lov-ede,	They lov-eden, lov-ede

The MSS. of Chaucer's poetical works frequently have *loved*, those of his prose very rarely.

In some, as the Harl. MS., we find *has* for *hast*, *dos* for *dost*, an evidence of the influence of the Northumbrian, in which the 2nd pers. sing. ended in -*es*, and we sometimes meet with the termination -*eth* in the 3rd plur. pres., simulating the singular, owing to the fact of that being the plural inflexion of all three persons in the southern counties = -*ath* in A. Sax.

> " And over his heed ther *schyneth* two figures."
> Knightes Tale, 1185, Harl. MS.

We often find -*th* for -*eth*, as *spekth* for *speketh.*

Saxon verbs whose roots end in -*d*, -*t*, and rarely in -*s*, are contracted in the 3rd sing. pres., as *sit* for *sitteth*, *writ* for *writeth*, *halt* for *holdeth*, *fint* for *findeth*, *stont* for *stondeth* (stands), and *rist* for *riseth*.

II. Some verbs of the weak conjugation form the past tense by adding -*dĕ* or -*tĕ* instead of -*ede*, as *heren*, *herdĕ*; *hiden*, *hiddĕ*; *kepen*, *keptĕ*; but if the root end in *d* or *t*, preceded by another consonant, -*ĕ* only is added instead of -*dĕ* and -*tĕ*, as *wenden*, *wendĕ*; *sterten*, *stertĕ*; *letten* (to hinder), *lettĕ*.

III. In some verbs forming a link between the weak and strong conjugations we have a change of the vowel root together with the addition of the suffix -*dĕ* or *tĕ*, as *sellen*, *solde*; *tellen*, *tolde*; *seche* (to seek), *soughte*; and others in which modern English has abandoned the vowel change, as *delen*, *daltĕ* (dealt); *leden*, *laddĕ* (led): *leven*, *laftĕ* (left).

THE STRONG VERBS

Are those which form the past tense by merely changing the root vowel, as *sterven*, to die, *starf*, and the past part. by the addition of -*en* or *ĕ*, besides a vowel change which may or may not be the same as in the past tense, as *storven* or *storvĕ* (O.E. *ystorven*). Cf. Ger. *sterben*, *starb*, *gestorben*.

The 1st and 3rd persons singular of the past tense had no final *e*, as printed in some modern editions; the three persons plural ended in -*en* or -*ĕ*, and the 2nd person singular in -*ĕ*, frequently dropped, or occasionally in -*est*.

Some strong verbs had two forms for the past tense, one simple and the other taking the suffix of weak verbs—

Present.	Past.
Weep,	wep or weptĕ.
Creep,	crep or creptĕ.

A number of the older verbs of this conjugation, in which the root vowel of the past participle was not the same as that of the past tense, employed it in the plural of the latter thus—

Sterven, past sing. *starf*,		p. plur. *storven;*	p. part. *(y)storven.*		
Riden,	„ ·	*rood* or *rod*,	„ *riden;*	„	*(y)riden.*
Smiten,	„	*smoot;*	„ *smiten;*	„	*(y)smiten.*

This difference between the numbers was soon lost.

SUBJUNCTIVE.

The present singular ends in *-e*, the plural in *-en*; the past singular in *-ede*, *-de*, or *-te*, the plural in *-eden*, *-den*, or *-ten*, in all the persons; except in a few such forms as *speke* we, *go* we.

IMPERATIVE.

The only inflections are an *-eth*, or occasionally an *-e* in the 2nd pers. plural; and in verbs conjugated like *tellen* and *loven*, an *-e* in the singular also.

THE INFINITIVE.

Originally the infinitive ended in *-en* (the Saxon *-an*), but the *-n* was often dropped, leaving an *-e* only, a change which began in the south.

The so-called gerund, really the objective (dative) case of the infinitive, and known by being preceded by *to*, in the sense of "for the purpose of," "in order to," &c., was formed from the former by adding *-e*, and must not in its full or contracted forms be confounded with the infinitive.

Ex. *to doon-e*=*to don-ne*. In Prol. 134, "no ferthing *sene*"=*for to senne*. In l. 720, "*for to telle*" is the gerund also, but the *-n* has been discarded.

The present participle usually ends in *-yng*, or *-ynge* when the rime demands it. Originally the participle ended in *-inde* or *-ind* in the south, *-ande* or *-and* (occasionally met with in Chaucer) in the north, both forms being employed in the east midland.

Verbal nouns were formed by the termination *-ung* or later *-ing,* and then the participles were assimilated to them by changing -*inde* and -*ind* into -*ynge*, -*yng*, or -*ing*, as in our present language.

The infinitive in -*an* or -*en* was also under certain circumstances reduced to the same termination -*ing*, and the several forms co-existing in our language present much difficulty to students.

The past participle of weak verbs ends in -*ed* or -*d*, or occasionally in -*et* or -*t*; of strong verbs in -*en* or -*e*, with change of the root vowel in some, and they are all sometimes preceded by the old prefix *y-*, *i-* (A.S. *ge-*), as *i-ronne*, *i-falle*, *y-clept*.

ANOMALOUS VERBS.

Those whose inflexions cannot be brought under any rule, some of which are defective, and others, as *to go*, whose wanting parts are made up by borrowing the corresponding members of others, are the truly *irregular* verbs. This name has also been most unhappily given by grammarians trained in the schools of Greek and Latin to those of the strong conjugation because they are the most removed from the inflectional systems of those languages; whereas they are the most characteristic of the Teutonic family, and in that sense the more regular. Words taken from the Latin are thus instinctively in every instance referred to the weak conjugation as the less peculiarly Teutonic of the two.

1. *Ben, been,* to be; 1st sing. pres. ind. *am;* 2nd, *art;* 3rd, *is;* plur. *been, aren, are;* past, *was, wast, was,* and *were;* imp. sing. *be,* pl. *beth;* p. part. *ben, been.*

This, the "verb substantive," is in fact made up of portions of three distinct verbs, which long coexisted in different dialects or even in the same so late as the seventeenth century, as may be seen in the A.V. of the Bible and in Milton, and to this day among the peasantry.

2. *Conne,* to know or to be able; pres. ind., 1st, *can;* 2nd, *can* or *canst;* 3rd, *can;* pl. *connen, conne;* past, 1st and 3rd, *couthe, cowthe, cowde;* p.p. *couth, coud.* The *l* in the modern word has been inserted through a false analogy with *would* and *should.*

3. *Darren, dare;* pres. ind., *dar, darst, dar;* pl. *dar, dorre;* past, *dorste, durste.*

4. *May;* pres. ind. sing., 1st and 3rd, *may, mow;* 2nd, *mayst* or *maist;* pl. *mowen, mowe;* pres. subj. *mowe;* past tense, 1st and 3rd, *mighte, moghte.*

5. *Mot,* must, may; ind. pres. sing., 1st and 3rd, *mot, moot;* 2nd *must, moot;* pl. *mooten, moote;* past tense, *moste.*

6. *Owen*, to owe (moral obligation); pres. *oweth;* past, *oughte, aughte;* pl. *oughten, oughte.*

7. *Schal*, shall (compulsion); pres. ind. sing., 1st and 3rd, *schal;* 2nd, *schalt;* pl. *schullen, schuln, s. hul;* past, *schulde, scholde.*

8. *Thar*, need (Ger. *dürfen*); pres. ind. sing. *thar;* past, *thurte;* subj. 3rd, *ther.*

9. *Witen*, to know; pres. ind. sing., 1st and 3rd, *wat, wot;* 2nd, *wost;* pl. *witen, wite; woote;* past, *wiste.*

10. *Wil*, will; pres. ind. sing., 1st, *wille, wil, wolle, wol;* 2nd, *wilt, wolt;* 3rd, *wile, wole, wol;* pl. *woln, willen, wille;* past, *wolde.*

It has the full meaning of the Latin *volo, e.g.* "Owre swete Lord of heven, that no man *wil perische*" (i.e. *neminem vult perdere*), Persones Tale.

NEGATIVE VERBS.

Nam = am not.	*Nylle, nyl* = will not.
Nys = is not.	*Nolde* = would not.
Nas = was not.	*Nat, not, noot* = knows not.
Nere = were not.	*Nost* = knowest not.
Nath = hath not.	*Nyste, nysten* = knew not.
Nadde, nade = had not.	

ADVERBS.

1. Adverbs are formed from adjectives by adding -*ĕ* to the latter, as *brightĕ*, brightly; *deepĕ*, deeply; *lowĕ*, lowly. This is the explanation of the seeming use of the adjective for the adverb in modern English, and which is called by some grammarians the "flat adverb."

2. Others are formed as now by adding -*lyche* or -*ly*, as *schortly, rudelyche, pleynly.*

3. And a few have *e* before the -*ly*, as *boldĕly, trewĕly, softĕly.*

4. Some end in -*en* or -*e*, as *aboven, aborĕ; abouten, aboutĕ; withouten, withoutĕ; siththen, siththĕ*, since. Many have dropped the -*n*, retaining the -*e* only, as *asondre, behyndĕ, bynethĕ, biyondĕ, bytwenĕ, hennĕ* (hence), *thennĕ* (thence), *oftĕ* in Chaucer, though *often* is the more usual form at present, *seldĕ* (seldom), *soonĕ.*

5. Adverbs in -*es*: *needes*, needs; *ones*, once; *twies* or *twie*, twice; *thries, thrie*, thrice; *unnethes*, scarcely; *whiles, bysides, togideres; hennes*, hence; *thennes*, thence; *whennes*, whence; *agaynes, ayens*, against; *amonges*, among, amongst; *amyddes*, amidst.

6. *Of-newĕ*, anew, newly (cf. *of yore, of late*); *as-now*, at present;

on slepĕ, asleep (fell *on sleep,* A.V. Acts xiii. 36) (cf. *on honting,* a hunting, &c.).

7. *There* and *then* occasionally stand for *where* and *when.*

8. *As,* used before *in, to, for, by,* = considering, with respect to, so far as concerns.

<blockquote>" As in so litel space." Prol. 87.</blockquote>

As is used before the imperative in supplicatory phrases—

<blockquote>" As keep me fro thi vengeaunce and thin yre." K. T. 1444.
" As sendĕ love and pees betwixe hem two." K. T. 1459.</blockquote>

(Cf. use of *que* in French.)

9. *But,* only (be-out) takes a negative before it. "I *nam but* deed." K. T. 416. Cf. again the French, "Je ne suis que . . ."

10. Two or more negatives do not make an affirmative. This is the usage of the A.S., and still holds its ground among "uneducated" persons.

<blockquote>" He *nevere* yit *no* vileinye *ne* sayde
In al his lyf unto *no* maner wight." Prol. 70, 71.</blockquote>

PREPOSITIONS.

Occasionally *til* = to (cf. the German *bis*), *unto* = until, *up* = upon, and *uppon* = on.

CONJUNCTIONS.

Ne . . . ne = neither . . . nor; *other . . . other* = either . . . or (cf. Ger. *oder*); *what . . . and* = both . . . and.

THE FINAL E.

The use and meaning of the final *e* in the several parts of speech may be thus summed up.

In many nouns and adjectives it represents the Anglo-Saxon terminations in *-a, -e,* or *-u,* and is then always sounded: *assĕ* and *cuppĕ* = A.S. *assa* and *cuppa; hertĕ* and *marĕ* = A.S. *heorte* and *mare; halĕ* and *wodĕ* = A.S. *healu* and *wudu; derĕ* and *dryĕ* = A.S. *deore* and *drygge.*

It is sounded when it stands as the sign of the objective indirect (or dative) case, as *rootĕ, breethĕ, heethĕ* (Prol. 2, 5, 6), and in *beddĕ* and *briggĕ,* from *bed* and *brig.*

It is sounded when it marks—

(*a*) The definite form of the adjective, "the *yongĕ* sonne." Prol. 7.

(*b*) The plural of adjectives, "*smalĕ* fowles." Prol. 9.

(*c*) The vocative of adjectives, "O *strongĕ* god!" K. T. 1515.

In verbs it is sounded when it represents the older termination -*en* or -*an* as a sign of—

(*a*) The infinitive, as to "*seekĕ, tellĕ.*" Prol. 17, 38.

(*b*) The "gerund," as "*senĕ.*" Prol. 134.

(*c*) The past participle, as "*i-ronnĕ, i-fallĕ.*" Prol. 8, 25.

(*d*) And in the past tenses of weak verbs in -*de* or -*te*, as *wentĕ, cowdĕ, woldĕ, feddĕ, weptĕ.*

It is sounded in adverbs where it—

(*a*) Represents older vowel-endings, as *sonĕ, twiĕ, thriĕ.*

(*b*) Marks the adverb from the corresponding adjective, as *fairĕ, riyhtĕ* = fairly, rightly.

(*c*) When it stands for the O.E. -*en*, A.S. *an*: *aboutĕ, abovĕ*, O.E. *abouten, aboven*, A.S. *abutan, abufan.*

(*d*) When followed by -*ly* in the double adverbial ending -*ĕly*, as *hertĕly, lustĕly, semĕly, trewĕly.*

It is silent in the past tenses of weak verbs in -*ede*, = *ed*, as *lovede.* Prol. 97.

It is mostly silent in—

(*a*) The personal pronouns *oure, youre, hire, here.*

(*b*) And in many words of more than two syllables.

The final unaccented *e* in words of French origin is generally silent, but often sounded as in French verse. The scanning of each particular line must decide.

VERSIFICATION.

The poetry of the Greeks and Romans was purely metrical. In their languages the distinction between long and short vowels was strongly marked, and the lines were composed of a definite number of feet, the feet consisting of two or more syllables long or short following one another in a regular order. Rimes when they occurred accidentally were looked on as faults.

In the later and debased age of the Latin language, when the pronunciation became corrupted, the regular metres gave way to verses composed of a fixed number of syllables, guided by accent rather than quantity, and with rimes in regular order.

This form of versification first appears in the later Latin hymns of the Western Church, and was adopted from the first in the poetry of the Romance languages.

Quite different was the verse employed by the early Germanic and Scandinavian poets, its distinctive feature being alliteration. Two more or less emphatic words in the first,. and one in the second line of each couplet began with the same consonant.

In the north and west of England the alliterative verse held its ground so late as the fifteenth century, but in the southern and eastern shires the riming verse was employed in the thirteenth.

The *Vision of Piers Plowman* (A.D. 1362) is a good example of alliterative verse.

> " I was *weori* of *wandringe,*
> And *went* me to reste
> Under a *brod banke*
> Bi a *bourne* syde.
> And as I *lay* and *leonede*
> And *lokede* on the watres,
> I *slumberde* in a *slepynge,*
> Hit *sownede* so murie."

In this extract the words in italics constitute the alliteration, the others, as *was* in the first, *Bi* in the fourth, and *so* in the last, are unemphatic, and contain the characteristic letter of each couplet only by accident.

Chaucer, a man of general culture, living in the south-eastern counties, and familiar with the poetry of Italy and France, naturally chose the metrical and riming style of verse.

His *Canterbury Tales* (except those of Melibeus and the Persone, which are in prose) are written in what is commonly called the heroic couplet. The lines consist of ten syllables, of which the second, fourth, sixth, eighth, and tenth are accented, or as the classical scholar would express it, they consist of five iambs. Very often, oftener indeed than is noticed by the ordinary reader, there is an eleventh and unaccented syllable at the end, the verse being then identical with iambic trimeter catalectic of the Greek and Latin poets; and far more rarely there are but nine syllables, an unaccented odd syllable beginning the line, and followed by four iambs.

To take a few unequivocal examples from the Prologue. The typical verse is seen in ll. 19, 20—

> Byfel | that in | that se | soun on | a day,
> In South | werk at | the Tab | ard as | I lay.

The verse of eleven syllables in ll. 11, 12—

> So prik | eth hem | nature | in here | corag | es,
> Thanne long | en folk | to gon | on pil | grimag | es.

And that of nine in l. 391—

> In ¦ a gowne | of fal | dyng to | the kne.

The opening couplet, though generally read as decasyllabic, is really composed of eleven, as will be seen by a reference to the grammar of Chaucer—

> Whan that | April | lĕ with | his schow | res swoot | ĕ,
> The drought | of Marche | hath per | ced to | the root | ĕ.

The word *nonĕs*, our *nonce*, must be read as a dissyllable in l. 523, or it would not rime with *non is* in that following, and in ll. 21, 22, *pilgrimagĕ* and *coragĕ* are probably to be read as in French poetry, the third syllable lightly sounded. So in the Parson's Prologue, l. 17, 345, Wright's ed.—

> "Do you | plesaun | cĕ le | ful as | I can."

Short unemphatic syllables are often slurred over, or two such consecutive syllables pronounced almost as one. These contractions may be arranged under several distinct heads.

1. That which has entered so largely into our spoken language, by which *wandering* and *wanderer* are pronounced *wand'ring* and *wand'rer*, *camest* as *cam'st*, &c.

2. The synalœpha of classic prosodists, or elision of a final vowel before another word beginning with a vowel or a silent *h*. This was far more frequent in our early poetry than is generally known, and often practised by Milton in his *Paradise Lost*.

3. A method of obliterating a short syllable which is of very common occurrence in Chaucer, though, as it seems to me, inadequately explained even by Dr. Morris and other equally eminent commentators. *The final consonant of a word ending with a short syllable is in reading to be attached to the initial vowel of the next.* It will be observed that in the great majority of contractions the following word begins with a vowel giving a clue to the proper reading.

Examples of the first are—

> " And *thinketh* ' here *cometh* ¦ my mor | tel en | emy." K. T. 785.
> " Sche gad | *ereth* flour ës par | ty white ¦ and rede." K. T. 195.
> " *Schuln* the | declar ¦ en, or | that thou | go henne." K. T. 1493.

Of the second or synalœpha àre—

> "And cer | tes lord | *to abi* ¦ den your presence." K. T. 69.
> " What schulde | he stud | *ie and* make | himsel | ven wood." Prol. 184.

Besides countless elisions of the terminal *e* which would have been sounded had the next word begun with a consonant.

Synæresis, or the blending of two vowels in the middle of a word, is seen in—

> " Ne stud | *ieth* nat; | ley hand | to ev ¦ ery man." Prol. 841.

Where *every* is also contracted after the first method into two syllables.

It is scarcely possible to scan a dozen lines without meeting an instance of the third mode of contraction, but a few examples may be given here—

> " And forth | we *ride* | n a lit | el more | than pass." Prol. 819.
> " And won | derly | de*lyve* | r and gret ' of strengthe." Prol. 84.
> " As an | y rav | ens *fethe* | r it schon | for blak." K. T. 1286.
> " A man | to light | a *cande* | l at his | lanterne."
> Cant. Tales, 1. 5961, Wright's edition.
> " And though | that I | no *wepe* | n have in | this place." K. T. 733.
> Thou schul | dest *neve* | re out of | this grov | ë pace." K. T. 744.

Whether is frequently sounded as a single syllable, and is sometimes written *wher*.

> " I not | *whether* sche | be wom | man or | godesse." K. T. 243.
> " Ne rec | cheth nev | ere wher | I synke | or fleete." K. T. 1539.

Words borrowed from the French ending in *-le* or *-re* are pronounced as in that language, with the final *e* mute: *table, temple, miracle, noble, propre, chapitre,* as *tabl', templ', miràcl', nobl', propr', chapitr';* and those of more than one syllable ending in *-ance* (*-aunce*), *-ence, -oun, -ie* (*-ige*), *-er, -ere, -age, -une, -ure,* and *-lle,* are generally accented on the last syllable (not counting the silent *e*), as *acqueyntaùnce, resoùn, manère, arauntàge,* &c.; but occasionally the accent is thrown back as in modern English, *e.g. bàttaille,* K. T.

21; *máner*, Prol. 71; *fórtune*, each of these words being elsewhere accented on the last syllable. Even some purely English words exhibit the same variety, as *hóntyng* and *huntýng*. K. T. 821 and 1450.

The -*ed* of past participles and the -*ede* of past tenses are to be alike pronounced as a distinct syllable, -*ed*; thus *percĕd*, Prol. l. 2, has two syllables, *entunĕd*, l. 123, *y-pinchĕd*, l. 151, have three, but *lovede*, l. 97, and similar forms, are to be sounded *lov-ĕd*, &c., with two, not three syllables.

The initial *h* in the several cases of the pronoun *he*, in the tenses of the verb *to have*, and in the word *how*, is so lightly sounded as to admit of the elision of a final -*e* before it.

> "Wel cowd*e* he dress*e* his takel yemanly." Prol. 106.

Both *e*'s would otherwise be sounded.

In all other words the initial *h* is too strongly aspirated to permit of this.

Not only is the negative *ne* frequently shortened into an initial *n*-before *am*, *is*, *hadde*, [*nadde*], *wot*, [*not*], &c., but we meet with such contractions as *thass* for *the asse*, *tabiden* for *to abiden*, &c. This may be merely due to the scribes. Cf. Prol. 450, where we have the elision in reading though not in the text.

The metrical analysis of the first eighteen lines of the Prologue, given in p. 37, will be found to illustrate most of the foregoing rules of prosody, and will serve as a guide to the correct scanning of Chaucer's verse, which when read as it should be will be found as smooth and regular in its rhythm as any of the present day.

In order to mark the pronunciation without deviating from the orthography of the best MSS. I have in this passage, as in the text generally, adopted the following simple devices and signs.

The final *e* when naturally silent, or when, as in the words *he*, *the*, &c., there can be no doubt as to its pronunciation, is printed in small romans; when, on the other hand, it is to be sounded where it is either silent or omitted in modern English, it is distinguished thus -*ĕ*; and where an *e* which would be sounded under other circumstances is elided before a word beginning with a vowel or lightly aspirated *h*, it will be found in italics.

Other vowels likewise when elided, whether by synalœpha or by any of the contractions explained above, are marked by italics.

If at the same time it be borne in mind that the finals -*es*, -*en*, and

-ed, being *Saxon* inflections, are, unless the contrary be indicated as above, to be sounded as distinct syllables, and that the *-ede* of the past tense is to be pronounced *-ed*, and that, with the exception of the few nine-syllabled verses, every line is either a perfect or a catalectic iambic, a little practice will enable the student to scan the poetry of Chaucer with ease.

A very few irregular contractions, either poetic licenses or anticipations of future pronunciations, may be found, as in Prol. 463. where "*thries hadde*" must be read as our "*thrice had.*"

"And thries | hadde sche | ben at | Jeru | salem."

I will conclude this section with a slightly altered transcription of Dr. Morris' remarks on the pronunciation and scanning of the passage on p. 37.

1. The final *e* in *Aprille* is sounded; but it is silent in the French words *veyne, vertue*, and *nature*, and in *Marche, holte*, and *kouthe*, because followed here by a vowel or lightly aspirated *h*.

2. The final *e* in *swoote, smale, straunge, ferne*, and *seeke* (in the last line) is sounded, as the sign of the plural.

3. The final *e* in *roote, breethe, heethe* is sounded, as the sign of the objective (indirect) case.

4. The final *e* in *swete, yonge, halfe* is sounded, as the definite form of the adjective.

5. The final *e* in *sonne, ende* is sounded, as representing older terminations.

6. The final *e* in *i-ronne* is sounded, as representing the old and fuller ending of the past participle *-en* (*y-ronnen*).

7. The final *e* in *wende* is sounded, as representing the *-en* of the plural.

8. And in *seeke* (l. 17), as the *-en* of the older infinitive.

    7*a*. The full forms of the plural are found in *slepen, maken, longen*, and

    8*a*. Of the infinitive in *seeken*, in all of which it is of course sounded.

9. The final *-es* in *schowres, croppes, fowles, halwes, strondes, londes*, is sounded as the inflexion of the plural; and

10. In *schires* as that of the possessive case.

11. *Vertue, licour, nature*, and *corages* are accented on the last syllable of the root, as being French words of comparatively recent introduction into English.

Whan that | April | lĕ with | his schow | res swoot | ĕ
The drought | of Marche | hath per | ced to | the root | ĕ,
And bath | ed eve | ry veyne | in swich | licour,
Of which | vertue | engen | dred is | the flour;
Whan Ze | phirus | eke with | his swe | tĕ breeth | ĕ
Enspir | ed hath | in eve | ry holte | and heeth | ĕ
The ten | dre crop | pes, and | the yong | ĕ sonn | ĕ
Hath in | the Ram | his hal | fĕ cours | i-ron | nĕ,
And smal | ĕ fowl | es mak | en mel | odi-e
That sle | pen al | the night | with o | pen eye,
So prik | eth hem | nature | in here | corag | es:—
Thanne long | en folk | to gon | on pil | grimag | es,
And palm | ers for | to seek | en straung | ĕ strond | es
To fer | ne hal | wes, kouthe | in son | dry lond | es;
And spe | cially, | from eve | ry schi | res end | ĕ
Of Eng | elond, | to Caunt | erbury | they wend | ĕ,
The ho | ly blis | ful mar | tir for | to seek | ĕ,
That hem | hath hol | pen whan | that they | were seek | ĕ.

The Knightes Tale, or at least a poem upon the same subject, was originally composed by Chaucer as a separate work. It is not impossible that at first it was a mere translation of the Teseide of Boccaccio, and that its present form was given it when Chaucer determined to assign it the first place among his Canterbury Tales.*

---

* "The Knight's Tale is an abridged translation of a part of Boccaccio's Teseide, but with considerable change in the plan, which is, perhaps, not much improved, and with important additions in the descriptive and the more imaginative portions of the story. These additions are not inferior to the finest parts of Boccaccio's work; and one of them, the description of the Temple of Mars, is particularly interesting, as proving that Chaucer possessed a power of treating the grand and terrible, of which no modern poet but Dante had yet given an example." (Marsh, Origin and History of the English Language, pp. 423, 424.) "Out of 2250 of Chaucer's lines, he has only translated 270 (less than one eighth) from Boccaccio; only 374 more lines bear a general likeness to Boccaccio; and only 132 more a slight likeness." (Furnivall.)

"Several parallel lines between Chaucer's Troilus and the Knightes Tale show that Troilus and the original draft of the Knightes Tale, to which Chaucer himself gives the name of 'Palemon,' were in hand at about the same time." (Skeat, in Notes and Queries, Fourth Series.)

It may not be unpleasing to the reader to see a short summary of it, which will show with what skill Chaucer has proceeded in reducing a poem of about ten thousand lines to a little more than two thousand without omitting any material circumstance.

The Teseide is distributed into twelve Books or Cantos.

Bk. I. Contains the war of Theseus with the Amazons, their submission to him, and his marriage with Hippolyta.

Bk. II. Theseus, having spent two years in Scythia, is reproached by Perithous in a vision, and immediately returns to Athens with Hippolyta and her sister Emilia. · He enters the city in triumph; finds the Grecian ladies in the temple of Clemenzia; marches to Thebes; kills Creon, &c., and brings home Palemone and Arcita, who are " Damnati—ad eterna presone."

Bk. III. Emilia, walking in a garden and singing, is heard and seen first by Arcita,* who calls Palemone. They are both equally enamored of her, but without any jealousy or rivalship. Emilia is supposed to see them at the window, and to be not displeased with their admiration. Arcita is released at the request of Perithous; takes his leave of Palemone, with embraces, &c.

Bk. IV. Arcita, having changed his name to *Pentheo*, goes into the service of Menelaus at Mycenæ, and afterwards of Peleus at Aegina. From thence he returns to Athens and becomes a favorite servant of Theseus, being known to Emilia, though to nobody else; till after some time he is overheard making his complaint in a wood, to which he usually resorted for that purpose, by Pamphilo, a servant of Palemone.

---

* In describing the commencement of this amour, which is to be the subject of the remainder of the poem, Chaucer has entirely departed from his author in three principal circumstances, and, I think, in each with very good reason: (1) By supposing Emilia to be seen first by Palemon, he gives him an advantage over his rival which makes the catastrophe more consonant to poetical justice; (2) the picture which Boccaccio has exhibited of two young princes violently enamored of the same object, without jealousy or rivalship, if not absolutely unnatural, is certainly very insipid and unpoetical; (3) as no consequence is to follow from their being seen by Emilia at this time, it is better, I think, to suppose, as Chaucer has done, that they are not seen by her.

Bk. V. Upon the report of Pamphilo, Palemone *begins* to be jealous of Arcita, and is desirous to get out of prison in order to fight with him. This he accomplishes. with the assistance of Pamphilo, by changing clothes with Alimeto, a physician. He goes armed to the wood in quest of Arcita, whom he finds sleeping. At first, they are very civil and friendly to each other. Then Palemone calls upon Arcita to renounce his pretensions to Emilia, or to fight with him. After many long expostulations on the part of Arcita, they fight, and are discovered first by Emilia, who sends for Theseus. When he finds who they are, and the cause of their difference, he forgives them, and proposes the method of deciding their claim to Emilia by a combat of a hundred on each side, to which they gladly agree.

Bk. VI. Palemone and Arcita live splendidly at Athens, and send out messengers to summon their friends, who arrive; and the principal of them are severally described, viz., Lycurgus, Peleus, Phocus, Telamon, &c.; Agamemnon, Menelaus, Castor, and Pollux, &c.; Nestor, Evander, Perithous, Ulysses, Diomedes, Pygmalion, Minos, &c.; with a great display of ancient history and mythology.

Bk. VII. Theseus declares the laws of the combat, and the two parties of a hundred on each side are formed. The day before the combat, Arcita, after having visited the temples of all the gods, makes a formal prayer to Mars. The prayer, *being personified*, is said to go and find Mars in his Temple in Thrace, which is described; and Mars, upon understanding the message, causes favorable signs to be given to Arcita. In the same manner Palemone closes his religious observances with a prayer to Venus. His prayer, *being also personified*, sets out for the temple of Venus on Mount Cithereone, which is also described; and the petition is granted. Then the sacrifice of Emilia to Diana is described, her prayer, the appearance of the goddess, and the signs of the two fires. In the morning they proceed to the theatre with their respective troops, and prepare for the action. Arcita puts up a private prayer to Emilia, and harangues his troop publicly, and Palemone does the same.

Bk. VIII. Contains a description of the battle, in which Palemone is taken prisoner.

Bk. IX. The horse of Arcita, being frighted by a Fury, sent from Hell at the desire of Venus, throws him. However, he is carried to Athens in a triumphal chariot with Emilia by his side; is put to bed dangerously ill; and there by his own desire espouses Emilia.

Bk. X. The funeral of the persons killed in the combat. Arcita, being given over by his physicians, makes his will, in discourse with Theseus, and desires that Palemone may inherit all his possessions and also Emilia. He then takes leave of Palemone and Emilia, to whom he repeats the same request. Their lamentations. Arcita orders a sacrifice to Mercury, which Palemone performs for him, and dies.

Bk. XI. Opens with the passage of Arcita's soul to heaven, imitated from the Ninth Book of Lucan. The funeral of Arcita. Description of the wood felled takes up six stanzas. Palemone builds a temple in honor of him, in which his whole history is painted. The description of this painting is an abridgment of the preceding part of the poem.

Bk. XII. Theseus proposes to carry into execution Arcita's will by the marriage of Palemone and Emilia. This they both decline for some time in formal speeches, but at last are persuaded and married. The kings, &c., take their leave, and Palemone remains—"in gioia e in diporto con la sua dona nobile e cortese."

THE KNIGHTES TALE.

WHILOM, as olde stories tellen us,
Ther was a duk that highte Theseus;
Of Athenes he was lord and governour,
And in his tyme swich a conquerour,
That gretter was ther non under the sonne.   5
Ful many a riche contré hadde he wonne;
That with his wisdam and his chivalric
He conquerede al the regne of Femenye,
That whilom was i-cleped Cithea;
And weddede he the queen Ipolita,   10
And broughte hire hoom with him in his contré
With mochel glorie and gret solempnité,
And eek hire yonge suster Emelye.
And thus with victorie and with melodye
Lete I this noble duk to Athenes ryde,   15
And al his host, in armes him biside.

---

3. *Governour.*—It should be observed that Chaucer continually accents
   words in the Norman-French manner, on the *last* syllable. Thus
   we have here *governóur;* again in the next line, *conqueróur;* in l. 7,
   chivalríe; in l. 11, *contré;* in l. 18, *manére,* &c. &c. The most re-
   markable examples are when the words end in *-oun* or *-ing* (ll. 25,
   26, 35, 36).
6. *Contré* is here accented on the *first* syllable; in l. 11, on the *last*. This
   is a good example of the unsettled state of the accents of such
   words in Chaucer's time, which afforded him an opportunity of
   license, which he freely uses.
7. *Chivalrie,* knightly exploits. In l. 20, *chivalrye* = knights; Eng. *chiv-
   alry.* So also in l. 124.
8. *Regne of Femenye.*—The kingdom of the Amazons. *Femenye* is from
   Lat. *fœmina,* a woman.
9. *Cithea,* Scythia.
10. *Ipolita,* Shakespeare's *Hippolyta,* in Mids. Night's Dream.

And certes, if it nere to long to heere,
I wolde han told *yow* fully the manere,
How wonnen was the regne of Femenye
By Theseus, and by his chivalrye;　　　　20
And of the grete bataille for the nones
Bytwixen Athenes and the Amazones;
And how aseged was Ypolita,
The faire hardy quen of Cithea;
And of the feste that was at hire weddynge,　　　　25
And of the tempest at hire hoom comynge;
But al that thing I mot as now forbere.
I have, God wot, a large feeld to ere,
And wayke ben the oxen in my plough,
The remenaunt of the tale is long inough;　　　　30
I wol not lette eek non of al this rowte,
Lat every felawe telle his tale aboute,
And lat see now who schal the soper wynne,
And ther I lafte, I wol agayn begynne.

This duk, of whom I make mencioun,　　　　35
Whan he was come almost unto the toun,
In al his wele and in his moste pryde,
He was war, as he caste his ey*gh*e aside,
Wher that ther knelede in the hye weye
A companye of ladies, tweye and tweye,　　　　40
Ech after other, clad in clothes blake;
But such a cry and such a woo they make,
That in this world nys creature lyvynge,
That herde such another weymentynge,
And of this cry they nolde nevere stenten,　　　　45
Til they the reynes of his bridel henten.

---

27. *As now*, at present, at this time.
31. *I wol not lette eek non of al this rowte*, I desire not to hinder eke (also) none of all this company.
43. *Creature* is a word of three syllables. ·
45. *Nolde*, would not: *ne wolde* was no doubt pronounced *nolde*, would not; so *ne hath*, hath not, was pronounced *nath.*
　　Stenten, stop. "She *stinted*, and cried aye." (Romeo and Juliet, i. 3. 48.)

"What folk ben *ye* that at myn hom comynge
Pertourben so my feste with cryinge?"
Quod Theseus, "have *ye* so gret envye
Of myn honour, that thus compleyne and crie?   50
Or who hath *yow* misboden, or offended?
And telleth me if it may ben amended;
And why that *ye* ben clothed thus in blak?"
   The eldeste lady of hem alle spak,
When sche hadde swowned with a dedly chere,   55
That it was routhe for to seen or heere;
And seyde: "Lord, to whom Fortune hath *yeven*
Victorie, and as a conquerour to lyven,
Nought greveth us *youre* glorie and honour;
But we beseken mercy and socour.   60
Have mercy on oure woo and oure distresse.
Som drope of pitee, thurgh thy gentilnesse,
Uppon us wrecchede wommen lat thou falle.
For certes, lord, ther nys noon of us alle,
That sche nath ben a duchesse or a queene;   65
Now be we caytifs, as it is wel seene:
Thanked be Fortune, and hire false wheel,
That noon estat assureth to ben weel.
And certes, lord, to abiden *youre* presence
Here in the temple of the goddesse Clemence   70
We han ben waytynge al this fourtenight;
Now help us, lord, syth it is in thy might.
I wrecche, which that wepe and waylle thus,
Was whilom wyf to kyng Capaneus,

---

50. *That thus*, i.e. *ye* that thus.
54. *Alle* is to be pronounced *al-lè*, but Tyrwhitt reads *than*, then, after
      alle.
55. *A dedly chere*, a deathly countenance.
60. *We beseken*, we beseech, ask for,   For such double forms as *beseken*
      and *besechen*, cf. mod. Eng. *sack* and *satchel*, *stick* and *stitch*.   In
      the Early Eng. period the harder forms with *k* were very frequent-
      ly employed by *Northern* writers, who preferred them to the·
      softer *Southern* forms (introduced by the Norman-French) with *ch*
68. This line means "that ensureth no estate to be good."
70. *Clemence*, clemency.
74. *Capaneus*, one of the seven heroes who besieged Thebes; struck deda

That starf at Thebes, cursed be that day,   75
And alle we that ben in this array,
And maken al this lamentacioun!
We losten alle oure housbondes at that toun,
Whil that the sege ther aboute lay.
And *yet* the olde Creon, welaway!   ·   80
That lord is now of Thebes the citee,
Fulfild of ire and of iniquité,
He for despyt, and for his tyrannye,
To do the deede bodyes vileinye,
Of alle oure lordes, whiche that ben i-slawe,   85
Hath alle the bodies on an heep y-drawe,
And wol not suffren hem by noon assent
Nother to ben y-buried nor y-brent,
But maketh houndes ete hem in despite."
And with that word, withoute more respite,   90
They fillen gruf, and criden pitously,
"Have on us wrecchede wommen som mercy,
And lat oure sorwe synken in thyn herte."
This gentil duk doun from his courser sterte
With herte pitous, whan he herde hem speke.   95
Him thoughte that his herte wolde breke,
Whan he seyh hem so pitous and so maat,
That whilom weren of so gret estat.
And in his armes he hem alle up hente,
And hem conforteth in ful good entente;   100
And swor his oth, as he was trewe knight,
He wolde don so ferforthly his might   ˎ

by lightning as he was scaling the walls of the city, because he had
defied Zeus.

83. *For despyt*, out of vexation.
84. *To do the deede bodyes vileinye*, to treat the dead bodies shamefully.
90. *Withoute more respite*, without longer delay.
91. *They fillen gruf*, they fell flat with the face to the ground.
96. *Him thoughte*, it seemed to him; cf. *methinks*, it seems to me. In O.
E. the verbs *like, list, seem, rue* (pity), are used impersonally. Cf.
the modern expression "if you please" = if it be pleasing to you.
97. *Maat*, dejected.
102. *Ferforthly*, i e. *far-forth-like*, to such an extent, as far as.

Upon the tyraunt Creon hem to wreke,
That al the people of Grece scholde speke
How Creon was of Theseus y-served, 105
As he that hadde his deth ful wel deserved.
And right anoon, withoute more abood
His baner he desplayeth, and forth rood
To Thebes-ward, and al his hoost bysyde;
No nerre Athenes wolde he go ne ryde, 110
Ne take his eese fully half a day,
But onward on his way that nyght he lay;
And sente anoon Ypolita the queene,
And Emelye hire yonge suster schene,
Unto the toun of Athenes to dwelle; 115
And forth he ryt; ther is no more to telle.
   The reede statue of Mars with spere and targe
So schyneth in his white baner large,
That alle the feeldes gliteren up and doun;
And by his baner born is his pynoun 120
Of gold ful riche, in which ther was i-bete
The Minatour which that he slough in Crete.
Thus ryt this duk, thus ryt this conquerour,
And in his hoost of chevalrie the flour,
Til that he cam to Thebes, and alighte 125
Faire in a feeld ther as he thoughte fighte.
But schortly for to speken of this thing,
With Creon, which that was of Thebes kyng,
He faught, and slough him manly as a knight
In pleyn bataille, and putte the folk to flight; 130
And by assaut he wan the cité after,
And rente adoun bothe wal, and sparre, and rafter;
And to the ladies he restorede agayn
The bones of here housbondes that were slayn,

---

107. *Abood*, delay, awaiting, abiding.
108. *His baner he desplayeth*, i.e. he summoneth his troops to assemble
   for military service.
110. *No nerre*, no nearer.
119. *Feeldes*, field, in an heraldic term for the ground upon which the
   various charges, as they are called, are emblazoned.
130. *In pleyn bataille*, in open or fair fight.

To don obsequies, as was tho the gyse.   135
But it were al to long for to devyse
The grete clamour and the waymentynge
Which that the ladies made at the brennynge
Of the bodyes, and the grete honour
That Theseus the noble conquerour   140
Doth to the ladyes, whan they from him wente.
But schortly for to telle is myn entente.
Whan that this worthy duk, this Theseus,
Hath Creon slayn, and wonne Thebes thus,
Stille in that feelde he took al night his reste,   145
And dide with al the contré as him leste.
    To ransake in the tas of bodyes dede
Hem for to streepe of herneys and of wede,
The pilours diden businesse and cure,
After the bataille and disconfiture.   150
And so byfil, that in the tas thei founde,
Thurgh-girt with many a grevous blody wounde,
Two yonge knightes liggyng by and by,
Bothe in oon armes, wroght ful richely;
Of whiche two, Arcite highte than oon,   155
And that other knight highte Palamon.
Nat fully quyke, ne fully deede they were,
But by here coote-armures, and by here gere,
The heraudes knewe hem best in special,
As they that weren of the blood real   160
Of Thebes, and of sistren tuo i-born.
Out of·the taas the pilours han hem torn,

---

135. *Obsequies,* accented on the *second* syllable.
146. *As him leste,* as it pleased him.
147. *Tas,* heap, collection.
152. *Thurgh-girt,* pierced through.
153. *Liggyng by and by,* lying separately. In later English, *by and by* signifies presently, immediately, as "the end is not *by and by.*"
154. *In oon armes,* in one (kind of) arms or armor, showing that they belonged to the same house.
157. *Nat fully quyke,* not wholly alive.
158. *By here coote-armures,* by their coat-armor, by the devices on the armor covering the breast.
    By here gere, by their *gear,* i.e. equipments.

And han hem caried softe unto the tente
Of Theseus, and he ful sone hem sente
Tathenes, for to dwellen in prisoun   165
Perpetuelly, he nolde no raunsoun.
And whan this worthy duk hath thus i-doon,
He took his host, and hom he ryt anoon
With laurer crowned as a conquerour;
And there he lyveth in joye and in honour   170
Terme of his lyf; what nedeth wordes moo?
And in a tour, in angwisch and in woo,
This Palamon, and his felawe Arcite,
For everemore, ther may no gold hem quyte.

   This passeth yeer by yeer, and day by day,   175
Til it fel oones in a morwe of May
That Emelie, that fairer was to seene
Than is the lilie on hire stalke grene,
And fresscher than the May with floures newe—
For with the rose colour strof hire hewe,   180
I not which was the fayrere of hem two—
Er it were day, as was hire wone to do,
Sche was arisen, and al redy dight;
For May wole han no sloggardye anight.
The sesoun priketh every gentil herte,   185
And maketh him out of his sleep to sterte,
And seith, "Arys, and do thin observaunce."
This makede Emelye han remembraun   ce
To don honour to May, and for to ryse.
I-clothed was sche fresshe for to devyse.   190
Hire yelwe heer was browded in a tresse,
Byhynde hire bak, a yerde long I gesse.

---

165. *Tathenes*, to Athens.
166. *He nolde no raunsoun*, he would accept of no ransom.
171. *Terme of his lyf*, the remainder of his life.
180. *Strof hire hewe*, strove her hue, i.e. her complexion contested the
    superiority with the rose's color.
181. *I not*, I know not; *not = ne wot*.
189. *May.*—See also l. 642.
191. *Hire yelwe heer was browded*, her yellow hair was braided.

And in the gardyn at the sonne upriste
Sche walketh up and doun, and as hire liste
Sche gadereth floures, party whyte and reede,   195
To make a sotil gerland for hire heede,
And as an aungel hevenlyche sche song.
The grete tour, that was so thikke and strong,
Which of the castel was the cheef dongeoun,
(Ther as the knightes weren in prisoun,   •   200
Of which I tolde *yow*, and telle schal)
Was evene joynant to the gardyn wal,
Ther as this Emelye hadde hire pleyynge.
Bright was the sonne, and cleer that morwenynge,
And Palamon, this woful prisoner,   205
As was his wone, by leve of his gayler
Was risen, and romede in a chambre on heigh,
In which he al the noble cité seigh,
And eek the gardyn, ful of braunches grene,
Ther as this fresshe Emely the scheene   210
Was in hire walk, and romede up and doun.
This sorweful prisoner, this Palamon,
Gooth in the chambre, romyng to and fro,
And to himself compleynyng of his woo;
That he was born, ful ofte he seyde, alas !   215
And so byfel, by aventure or cas,
That thurgh a wyndow thikke, of many a barre
Of iren greet, and squar as eny sparre,
He caste his eyen upon Emelya,
And therwithal he bleynte and cryede, a' !   220

193. *The sonne upriste*, the sun's uprising.
194. *As hire liste*, as it pleased her.
195. *Party*, partly.
196. *Sotil gerland*, a subtle garland; subtle has here the exact force of
    the Lat. *subtilis*, finely woven.
202. *Evene joynant*, closely joining, or adjoining.
203. *Ther as this Emelye hadde hire pleyynge*, i.e. where she was
    amusing herself.
216. *By aventure or cas*, by adventure or hap.
218. *Sparre*, a square wooden bolt; the bars, which were of iron, were a
    thick as they must have been if wooden. See l. 132.
220. *Bleynte*, the past tense of *blenche*, or *blenke* (to blink), to start,
    draw back suddenly.

As though he stongen were unto the herte.
And with that crye Arcite anon up-sterte,
And seyde, "Cosyn myn, what eyleth the,
Thou art so pale and deedly on to see?
Why crydestow? who hath the doon offence?   225
For Goddes love, tak al in pacience
Oure prisoun, for it may non other be;
Fortune hath yeven us this adversité
Som wikke aspect or disposicioun
Of Saturne, by sum constellacioun,   230
Hath yeven us this, although we hadde it sworn;
So stood the heven whan that we were born;
We moste endure it: this is the schort and pleyn."
      This Palamon answerde, and seyde ageyn,
"Cosyn, for sothe of this opynyoun   235
Thou hast a veyn ymaginacioun.
This prisoun causede me not for to crye.
But I was hurt right now thurghout myn eye
Into myn herte, that wol my bane be.
The fairnesse of that lady that I see   240
Yond in the gardyn rome to and fro,
Is cause of al my crying and my wo.
I not whether sche be womman or goddesse;
But Venus is it, sothly as I gesse."
And therwithal on knees adoun he fil,   245
And seyde: "Venus, if it be thy wil
Yow in this gardyn thus to transfigure,
Biforn me sorweful wrecche creature,
Out of this prisoun help that we may scape.
And if so be my destiné be schape   250

229. *Som wikke aspect.* See ll. 470, 1576, 1611.
233. *The schort and pleyn,* the brief and manifest statement of the case.
243. *Whether,* to be pronounced *wher,* which is a common form for
      whether.
247. *Yow* (used reflexively), yourself.
248. *Wrecche,* wretched, is a word of two syllables, like *wikke,* wicked,
      where the *d* is later and unnecessary addition.
250. *Schape = schapen,* shaped, determined. "*Shapes* our ends." (Shake
      speare, Hamlet. v. 2. 10.)

By eterne word to deyen in prisoun,
Of oure lynage have sum compassioun,
That is so lowey-brought by tyrannye."
And with that word Arcite gan espye
Wher as this lady romede to and fro.   255
And with that sighte hire beauté hurte him so,
That if that Palamon was wounded sore,
Arcite is hurt as moche as he, or more.
And with a sigh he seyde pitously :
"The fressche beauté sleeth me sodeynly   260
Of hire that rometh in the yonder place ;
And but I have hire mercy and hire grace,
That I may seen hire atte leste weye,
I nam but deed ; ther nys no more to seye."
This Palamon, whan he tho wordes herde,   265
Despitously he lokede, and answerde :
"Whether seistow this in ernest or in pley ? "
"Nay," quod Arcite, " in ernest by my fey.
God help me so, me lust ful evele pleye."
This Palamon gan knytte his browes tweye :   270
" It nere," quod he, "to the no gret honour,
For to be fals, ne for to be traytour
To me, that am thy cosyn and thy brother
I-sworn ful deepe, and ech of us to other,
That nevere for to deyen in the payne,   275
Till that the deeth departe schal us twayne,

---

262. And except I have her pity and her favor.
263. *Atte leste weye*, at the least. Cf. *leastwise = at the leastwise ; leastwise.*
264. *I am not but* (no better than) *dead*, there is no more to say Chaucer
       uses *ne—but* much in the same way as the Fr. *ne—que.*
268. *By my fey*, by my faith, in good faith.
269. *Me lust ful evele pleye*, it pleases me very badly to play.
271. *It nere = it were not*, it would not be.
275. That never, even though it cost us a miserable death, a death by
       torture.
276. Till that death shall part us two. Cp. the ingenious alteration in
       the Marriage Service, where the phrase "till death us depart" was
       altered into "do part" in 1661.

Neyther of us in love to hyndren other,
Ne in non other cas, my leeve brother;
But that thou schuldest trewely forthren me
In every caas, and I schal forthren the. 280
This was thyn oth, and myn also certeyn;
I wot right wel, thou darst it nat withseyn.
Thus art thou of my counseil out of doute.
And now thou woldest falsly ben aboute
To love my lady, whom I love and serve, 285
And evere schal, til that myn herte sterve.
Now certes, false Arcite, thou schalt not so.
I lovede hire first, and tolde the my woo
As to my counseil, and my brother sworn
To forthre me, as I have told biforn. 290
For which thou art i-bounden as a knight
To helpe me, if it lay in thi might,
Or elles art thou fals, I dar wel sayn."
This Arcite ful proudly spak agayn.
"Thou schalt," quod he, "be rather fals than I. 295
But thou art fals, I telle the utterly.
For *par amour* I lovede hire first er thow.
What wolt thou sayn? thou wistest not *y*it now
Whether sche be a womman or goddesse.
Thyn is affeccioun of holynesse, 300
And myn is love, as to a creature;
For which I tolde the myn aventure
As to my cosyn, and my brother sworn.
I pose, that thou lovedest hire biforn;

---

278. *Cas*, case. It properly means event, hap. See l. 216.
My leeve brother, my dear brother.
283. *Out of doute*, without doubt, doubtless.
289. *Counseil*, advice. See l. 303.
293. *I dar wel sayn*, I dare maintain.
295. *Thou schalt be*. Chaucer occasionally uses *shall* in the sense of *owe*, so that the true sense of *I shall* is *I owe* (Lat. *debeo*); the sense is "Thou art sure to be false sooner than I am."
297. *Par amour*, with love, in the way of love. To love *par amour* is an old phrase for to love excessively.
300. *Affeccioun of holynesse*, a sacred affection, or aspiration after.
304. *I pose*, I put the case, I will suppose.

Wost thou nat wel the olde clerkes sawe,   305
That who schal *y*eve a lover eny lawe,
Love is a gretter lawe, by my pan,
Then may be *y*eve to eny erthly man ?
Therfore posityf lawe, and such decré,
Is broke alday for love in ech degrèe.   310
A man moot needes love maugre his heed.
He may nought flen it, though he schulde be deed,
Al be sche mayde, or widewe, or elles wyf.
And eek it is nat likly al thy lyf
To stonden in hire grace, no more schal I;   315
For wel thou wost thyselven verraily,
That thou and I been dampned to prisoun
Perpetuelly, us gayneth no raunsoun.
We stryve, as dide the houndes for the boon,
They foughte al day, and *y*it here part was noon ;   320
Ther com a kyte, whil that they were so wrothe,
And bar awey the boon bitwixe hem bothe.
And therfore at the kynges court, my brother,
Ech man for himself, ther is non other.
Love if the list ; for I love and ay schal ;   325
And sothly, leeve brother, this is al.
Here in this prisoun moote we endure,
And everych of us take his aventure."
Gret was the stryf and long bytwixe hem tweye
If that I hadde leyser for to seye ;   330
But to theffect.—It happede on a day,
(To telle it *y*ow as schortly as I may)   ˋ

---

305. Knowest thou not well the old writer's saying ? The *olde clerke* is
    Boethius, from whose book Chaucer has borrowed largely in
    many places. The passage alluded to is in lib. iii. met. 12:
       " Quis legem det amantibus ?
         Major lex amor est sibi."
309. *And such decré*, and (all) such ordinances.
310. *In ech degree*, in every rank of life.
314. *And eek it is*, &c., and moreover it is not likely that ever in all thy
    life thou wilt stand in her favor.
328. *Everych of us*, each of us, every one of us.
331. *To theffect*, to the result, or end.

A worthy duk that highte Perotheus,
That felawe was unto duk Theseus
Syn thilke day that they were children lyte,   335
Was come to Athenes, his felawe to visite,
And for to pleye, as he was wont to do,
For in this world he lovede no man so :
And he lovede him as tendrely agayn.
So wel they lovede, as olde bookes sayn,   340
That whan that oon was deed, sothly to telle,
His felawe wente and soughte him doun in helle ;
But of that story lyst me nought to write.
Duk Perotheus lovede wel Arcite,
And hadde him knowe at Thebes yeer by yeer ;   345
And fynally at requeste and prayer
Of Perotheus, withouten any raunsoun
Duk Theseus him leet out of prisoun,
Frely to gon, wher that him luste overal,
In such a gyse, as I you telle schal.   350
This was the forward, playnly for tendite,
Bitwixe Theseus and him Arcite :
That if so were, that Arcite were yfounde
Evere in his lyf, by daye or night, o stound
In eny contré of this Theseus,   355
And he were caught, it was acorded thus,
That with a swerd he scholde lese his heed ;
Ther nas noon other remedy ne reed,
But took his leeve, and homward he him spedde ;
Let him be war, his nekke lith to wedde.   360
    How gret a sorwe suffreth now Arcite !
The deth he feleth thurgh his herte smyte ;
He weepeth, weyleth, cryeth pitously ;
To slen himself he wayteth pryvely.

---

342. *In helle.* An allusion to Theseus accompanying Perithous in his
    expedition to carry off Proserpina, when both were taken
    prisoners, and Perithous was torn in pieces by the dog Cerberus.
354. *O stound,* one moment, any short interval of time.
360. *His nekke lith to wedde,* his neck is in jeopardy.
364. *To slen himself he wayteth pryvely,* he watches for an opportunity
    to slay himself unperceived.

He seyde, " Allas the day that I was born !   365
Now is my prisoun werse than biforn ;
Now is me schape eternally to dwelle
Nought in purgatorie, but in helle.
Allas ! that evere knew I Perotheus !
For elles hadde I dweld with Theseüs   370
I-fetered in his prisoun evere moo.
Than hadde I ben in blisse, and nat in woo.
Oonly the sighte of hire, whom that I serve,
Though that I nevere hire grace may deserve,
Wolde han sufficed right ynough for me.   375
O dere cosyn Palamon," quod he,
" Thyn is the victorie of this aventure,
Ful blisfully in prisoun maistow dure ;
In prisoun ? certes nay, but in paradys !
Wel hath fortune y-torned the the dys,   380
That hast the sighte of hire, and I thabsence.
For possible is, syn thou hast hire presence,
And art a knight, a worthi and an able,
That by som cas, syn fortune is chaungeable,
Thou maist to thy desir somtyne atteyne.   385
But I that am exiled, and bareyne
Of alle grace, and in so gret despeir,
That ther nys erthe, water, fyr, ne eyr,
Ne creature, that of hem maked is,
That may me helpe or doon confort in this.   390
Wel oughte I sterve in wanhope and distresse ;
Farwel my lyf, my lust, and my gladnesse.`
Allas, why pleynen folk so in commune
Of purveiaunce of God, or of fortune,
That yeveth hem ful ofte in many a gyse   395
Wel bettre than thei can hemself devyse ?

---

367. *Now is me schape*, now am I destined ; literally, now is it *shapen*
     (or appointed) for me.
379. *Paradys* must be pronounced as a word of two syllables (*parays*).
389. It was supposed that all things were made of the four elements
     mentioned l. 388. "Does not our life consist of the four elements ?"
     (Shakespeare, Twelfth Night, ii. 3. 10.)

Som man desireth for to han richesse,
That cause is of his morthre or gret seeknesse.
And som man wolde out of his prisoun fayn,
That in his hous is of his meyné slayn.   400
Infinite harmes ben in this mateere ;
We witen nat what thing we prayen heere.
We faren as he that dronke is as a mous,
A dronke man wot wel he hath an hous,
But he not which the righte wey is thider,   405
And to a dronke man the wey is slider,
And certes in this world so faren we ;
We seeken faste after felicité,
But we gon wrong ful ofte trewely.
Thus may we seyen alle, and namelyche I,   410
That wende and hadde a gret opinioun,
That yif I mighte skape fro prisoun,
Than hadde I ben in joye and perfyt hele,
Ther now I am exiled fro my wele.
Syn that I may not sen yow, Emelye,   415
I nam but deed ; ther nys no remedye."
   Uppon that other syde Palamon,
Whan that he wiste Arcite was agoon,
Such sorwe he maketh, that the grete tour
Resowneth of his yollyng and clamour.   420
The pure fettres on his schynes grete
Weren of his bittre salte teres wete.
" Allas !" quod he, " Arcita, cosyn myn,
Of al oure strif, God woot, the fruyt is thin.
Thou walkest now in Thebes at thi large,   425
And of my woo thou yevest litel charge.
Thow maist, syn thou hast wysdom and manhede,

---

399. And another man would fain (get) out of his prison.
401. *mateere*, in the *matter* of thinking to excel God's providence.
402. We never know what thing it is that we pray for here below. See
    Romans viii. 26.
403. *Dronke is as a mous*. The phrase seems to have given way to
    "drunk as a rat."
421. *Pure fettres*, the very fetters.
425. *At thi large*, at large.

Assemblen al the folk of oure kynrede,
And make a werre so scharpe on this cité,
That by som aventure, or som treté,   430
Thou mayst have hire to lady and to wyf,
For whom that I mot needes leese my lyf.
For as by wey of possibilité,
Syth thou art at thi large of prisoun free,   ·
And art a lord, gret is thin avauntage,   435
More than is myn, that sterve here in a kage.
For I moot weepe and weyle, whil I lyve,
With al the woo that prisoun may me yyve,
And eek with peyne that love me yeveth also,
That doubleth al my torment and my wo."   440
Therwith the fyr of jelousye upsterte
Withinne his breste, and hente him by the herte
So wodly, that he lik was to byholde
The box-tree, or the asschen deede and colde.
Tho seyde he; "O cruel goddes, that governe   445
This world with byndyng of youre word eterne,
And writen in the table of athamaunte
Youre parlement, and youre eterne graunte,
What is mankynde more unto yow holde
Than is the scheep, that rouketh in the folde?   450
For slayn is man right as another beest,
And dwelleth eek in prisoun and arreest,
And hath seknesse, and greet adversité,
And ofte tymes gilteles, pardé.
What governaunce is in this prescience,   '   455
That gilteles tormenteth innocence?
And yet encresceth this al my penaunce,
That man is bounden to his observaunce
For Goddes sake to letten of his wille,
Ther as a beest may al his lust fulfille.   460
And whan a beest is deed, he hath no peyne;
But man after his deth moot wepe and pleyne,
Though in this world he have care and woo:

---

444. White like box-wood, or ashen-gray.
459. *To letten of his wille*, to refrain from his will (or lusts).

Withouten doute it may stonde so.
The answere of this I lete to divinis,   465
But wel I woot, that in this world gret pyne is.
Allas ! I se a serpent or a theef,
That many a trewe man hath doon mescheef,
Gon at his large, and wher him lust may turne.
But I moot ben in prisoun thurgh Saturne,   470
And eek thurgh Juno, jalous and eek wood,
That hath destruyed wel neyh al the blood
Of Thebes, with his waste walles wyde.
And Venus sleeth me on that other syde
For jelousye, and fere of him Arcyte."   475
   Now wol I stynte of Palamon a lite,
And lete him in his prisoun stille dwelle,
And of Arcita forth I wol you telle.
The somer passeth, and the nightes longe
Encrescen double wise the peynes stronge   480
Bothe of the lovere and the prisoner.
I noot which hath the wofullere myster.
For schortly for to seyn, this Palamoun
Perpetuelly is dampned to prisoun,
In cheynes and in fettres to be deed;   485
And Arcite is exiled upon his heed
For evere mo as out of that contré,
Ne nevere mo he schal his lady see.
Yow loveres axe I now this questioun,
Who hath the worse, Arcite or Palamoun ?   490
That on may se his lady day by day,
But in prisoun he moste dwelle alway.
That other wher him lust may ryde or go,
But seen his lady schal he nevere mo.
Now deemeth as you luste, ye that can,   495
For I wol telle forth as I bigan.
   Whan that Arcite to Thebes comen was,
Ful ofte a day he swelte and seyde alas,
For seen his lady schal he nevere mo.

---

489. *This questioun.*—An implied allusion to the mediæval courts of
love, in which questions of this kind were seriously discussed.

And schortly to concluden al his wo,   500
So moche sorwe hadde nevere creature,
That is or schal whil that the world may dure.
His sleep, his mete, his drynk is him byraft,
That lene he wex, and drye as is a schaft.
His eyen holwe, and grisly to biholde;   505
His hewe falwe, and pale as asschen colde,
And solitarye he was, and evere allone,
And waillyng al the night, making his moone.
And if he herde song or instrument,
Then wolde he wepe, he mighte nought be stent;   510
So feble eek were his spiritz, and so lowe.
And chaunged so, that no man couthe knowe
His speche nother his vois, though men it herde.
And in his geere, for al the world he ferde
Nought oonly lyke the loveres maladye   515
Of Hereos, but rather lik manye
Engendred of humour malencolyk,
Byforen in his selle fantastyk.
And schortly turned was al up-so-doun
Bothe habyt and eek disposicioun   520
Of him, this woful lovere daun Arcite.
What schulde I alday of his wo endite?
Whan he endured hadde a yeer or tuo
This cruel torment, and this peyne and woo,
At Thebes, in his contré, as I seyde,   525
Upon a night in sleep as he him leyde,
Him thoughte how that the wenged god Mercurie
Byforn him stood, and bad him to be murye.
His slepy yerde in hond he bar uprighte;

---

508. *Making his moone*, making his complaint or *moan*.
514–517. And in his manner for all the world he conducted himself
not like one suffering from the lover's melancholy of Eros, but
rather (his disease was) like *mania* engendered of " humor melancholy."
518. *In his selle fantastyk*.—The division of the brain into cells, according to the different sensitive faculties, is very ancient, and is found
depicted in mediæval manuscripts. The *fantastic cell (fantasia)*
was in front of the head. (Wright.)

An hat he werede upon his heres brighte. 530
Arrayed was this god (as he took keepe)
As he was whan that Argus took his sleepe;
And seyde him thus:" To   Athenes schalt thou wende;
Ther is the schapen of thy wo an ende."
And with that word Arcite wook and sterte. 535
"Now trewly how sore that me smerte."
Quod he, "to Athenes right now wol I fare;
Ne for the drede of deth schal I not spare
To see my lady, that I love and serve;
In hire presence I recche nat to sterve.' 540
And with that word he caughte a gret myrour,
And saugh that chaunged was al his colour,
And saugh his visage al in another kynde.
And right anoon it ran him in his mynde.
That sith his face was so disfigured 545
Of maladie the which he hadde endured,
He mighte wel, if that he bar him lowe,
Lyve in Athenes evere more unknowe,
And seen his lady wel neih day by day.
And right anon he chaungede his aray, 550
And cladde him as a poure laborer.
And al allone, save oonly a squyer,
That knew his pryveté and al his cas,
Which was disgysed povrely as he was,
To Athenes is he gon the nexte way. 555
And to the court he wente upon a day,
And at the yate he profreth his servyse,   .
To drugge and drawe, what so men wol devyse.
And schortly of this matere for to seyn,
He fel in office with a chamberleyn, 560
The which that dwellyng was with Emelye.
For he was wys, and couthe sone aspye
Of every servaunt, which that serveth here.
Wel couthe he hewen woode, and water bere,

---

532. *Argus*, Argus of the hundred eyes, whom Mercury charmed to sleep
    before slaying him.
547. *Bar him lowe*, conducted himself as one of low estate,

For he was yong and mighty for the nones,   565
And therto he was strong and bygge of bones
To doon that eny wight can him devyse.
A yeer or two he was in this servise,
Page of the chambre of Emelye the brighte;
And Philostrate he seide that he highte.   570
But half so wel byloved a man as he
Ne was ther nevere in court of his degree.
He was so gentil of condicioun,
That thurghout al the court was his renoun.
They seyde that it were a charité   575
That Theseus wolde enhaunse his degree,
And putten him in worschipful servyse,
Ther as he mighte his vertu excercise.
And thus withinne a while his name is spronge
Bothe of his dedes, and his goode tonge,   580
That Theseus hath taken him so neer
That of his chambre he made him a squyer,
And yaf him gold to mayntene his degree;
And eek men broughte him out of his countré
Fro yeer to yeer ful pryvely his rente;   585
But honestly and sleighly he it spente,
That no man wondrede how that he it hadde.
And thre yeer in this wise his lyf he ladde,
And bar him so in pees and eek in werre,
Ther nas no man that Theseus hath derre.   590
And in this blisse lete I now Arcite,
And speke I wole of Palamon a lyte.
    In derknesse and horrible and strong prisoun
This seven yeer hath seten Palamoun,
Forpyned, what for woo and for distresse;   595
Who feleth double sorwe and hevynesse
But Palamon? that love destreyneth so,
That wood out of his wit he goth for wo;
And eek therto he is a prisoner
Perpetuelly, nat oonly for a yeer.   600

---

586. *Sleighly*, prudently, wisely.

Who couthe ryme in Englissch proprely
His martirdam? for sothe it am nat I;
Therfore I passe as lightly as I may.
Hit fel that in the seventhe yeer in May
The thridde night, (as olde bookes seyn,   605
That al this storie tellen more pleyn)
Were it by aventure or destiné,
(As, whan a thing is schapen, it schal be,)
That soone after the mydnyght, Palamoun
By helpyng of a freend brak his prisoun,   610
And fleeth the cité faste as he may goo,
For he hadde yive his gayler drinke soo
Of a clarré, maad of a certeyn wyn,
With nercotykes and opye of Thebes fyn,
That al that night though that men wolde him schake,
The gayler sleep, he mighte nought awake.   616
And thus he fleeth as faste as evere he may.
The night was schort, and faste by the day,
That needes-cost he moste himselven hyde,
And til a grove faste ther besyde   620
With dredful foot than stalketh Palamoun.
For schortly this was his opynyoun,
That in that grove he wolde him hyde al day,
And in the night then wolde he take his way
To Thebes-ward, his frendes for to preye   625
On Theseus to helpe him to werreye;
And schorteliche, or he wolde lese his lyf,
Or wynnen Emelye unto his wyf.
This is theffect and his entente playn.
Now wol I torne unto Arcite agayn,   630

605. The third night is followed by the fourth day; so Palamon and Ar-‑
    cite meet on the 4th of May (l. 715), which was a Friday (l. 676), and
    the first hour of which (l. 635) was dedicated to Venus (l. 678) and
    to lovers' vows (l. 643). (Skeat.)
613. *Clarré.* The French term *claré* seems simply to have denoted a
    clear transparent wine, but in its most usual sense a compound
    drink of wine with honey and spices, so delicious as to be compar-
    able to the necta orf the gods.
619. *Needes-cost,* for *needes coste,* by the force of necessity.

That litel wiste how nyh that was his care,
Til that fortune hadde brought him in the snare.
　　The busy larke, messager of daye,
Salueth in hire song the morwe graye;
And fyry Phebus ryseth up so brighte,   635
That al the orient laugheth of the lighte,
And with his stremes dryeth in the greves
The silver dropes, hongyng on the leeves.
And Arcite, that is in the court ryal
With Theseus, his squyer principal,   640
Is risen, and loketh on the merye day.
And for to doon his observaunce to May,
Remembryng on the poynt of his desir,
He on his courser, stertyng as the fir,
Is riden into the feeldes him to pleye,   645
Out of the court, were it a myle or tweye.
And to the grove, of which that I yow tolde,
By aventure his wey he gan to holde,
To maken him a garland of the greves,
Were it of woodebynde or hawethorn leves,   650
And lowde he song ayens the sonne scheene:
'May, with alle thy floures and thy greene,
Welcome be thou, wel faire fressche May,
I hope that I som grene gete may.'
And fro his courser, with a lusty herte,   655
Into the grove ful hastily he sterte,
And in a path he rometh up and doun,
Ther as by aventure this Palamoun
Was in a busche, that no man mighte him see,
For sore afered of his deth was he.   660
Nothing ne knew he that it was Arcite:
God wot he wolde han trowed it ful lite.
But soth is seyd, goon sithen many yeres,
That feld hath eyen, and the woode hath eeres.
It is ful fair a man to bere him evene,   665
For al day meteth men at unset stevene.

---

650. *Were it* = if it were only.
666. *At unset stevene*, at a meeting not previously fixed upon, an unexpected meeting or appointment.

Ful litel woot Arcite of his felawe,
That was so neih to herknen al his sawe,
For in the busche he sytteth now ful stille.
Whan that Arcite hadde romed al his fille,   670
And songen al the roundel lustily,
Into a studie he fel al sodeynly,
As don thes loveres in here queynte geeres,
Now in the croppe, now doun in the breres,
Now up, now doun, as boket in a welle.   675
Right as the Friday, sothly for to telle,
Now it schyneth, now it reyneth faste,
Right so gan gery Venus overcaste
The hertes of hire folk, right as hire day
Is gerful, right so chaungeeh sche array.   680
Selde is the Fryday al the wyke i-like.
Whan that Arcite hadde songe, he gan to sike,
And sette him doun withouten eny more:
' Alas!' quod he, ' that day that I was bore!
How longe Juno, thurgh thy cruelté,   685
Wiltow werreyen Thebes the citee?
Allas ! i-brought is to confusioun
The blood royal of Cadme and Amphioun;
Of Cadmus, which that was the firste man
That Thebes bulde, or first the toun bygan,   690
And of that cité first was crowned kyng,
Of his lynage am I, and his ofspring
By verray lyne, as of the stok ryal:
And now I am so caytyf and so thral,
That he that is my mortal enemy,   695
I serve him as his squyer povrely.
And yet doth Juno me wel more schame,
For I dar nought byknowe myn owne name,
But ther as I was wont to hote Arcite,
Now highte I Philostrate, nought worth a myte.   700

---

673. *Bere queynte geeres*, their strange behaviors.
674. Now in the top (i.e., elevated, in high spirits), now down in the
    briars (i.e., depressed, in low spirits).

Allas! thou felle Mars, allas! Juno,
Thus hath youre ire owre kynrede al fordo,
Save oonly me, and wrecched Palamoun,
That Theseus martyreth in prisoun.
And over al this, to sleen me utterly,   705
Love hath his fyry dart so brennyngly
I-styked thurgh my trewe careful herte,
That schapen was my deth erst than my scherte.
Ye slen me with youre eyen, Emelye;
Ye ben the cause wherfore that I dye.   710
Of al the remenant of myn other care
Ne sette I nought the mountaunce of a tare,
So that I couthe don aught to youre plesaunce. '
And with that word he fel doun in a traunce
A long tyme; and afterward he upsterte   715
This Palamon, that thoughte that thurgh his herte
He felte a cold swerd sodeynliche glyde;
For ire he quook, no lenger nolde he byde.
And whan that he hadde herd Arcites tale,
As he were wood, with face deed and pale.   720
He sterte him up out of the bussches thikke,
And seyde: 'Arcyte, false traitour wikke,
Now art thou hent, that lovest my lady so,
For whom that I have al this peyne and wo,
And art my blood, and to my counseil sworn,   725
As I ful ofte have told the heere byforn,
And hast byjaped here duk Theseus,
And falsly chaunged hast thy name thus;'
I wol be deed, or elles thou schalt dye.
Thou schalt not love my lady Emelye,   730
But I wil love hire oonly and no mo;
For I am Palamon thy mortal fo.
And though that I no wepne have in this place,
But out of prisoun am astert by grace,
I drede not that outher thou schalt dye,   735
Or thou ne schalt not loven Emelye.

---

735. *I drede not*, I have no fear, I doubt not.
735, 736. *Outher . . . or* = either . . . or.

Ches which thou wilt, for thou schalt not asterte.'
This Arcite, with ful despitous herte,
Whan he him knew, and hadde his tale herd,
As fers as lyoun pullede out a swerd, 740
And seide thus: "By God that sit above,
Nere it that thou art sik and wood for love,
And eek that thou no wepne hast in this place,
Thou schuldest nevere out of this grove pace,
That thou ne schuldest deyen of myn hond. 745
For I defye the seurté and the bond
Which that thou seyst that I have maad to the.
What, verray fool, think wel that love is fre!
And I wol love hire mawgre al thy might.
But, for as muche thou art a worthy knight. 750
And wilnest to derreyne hire by batayle,
Have heer my trouthe, to-morwe I nyl not fayle,
Withouten wityng of eny other wight,
That heer I wol be founden as a knight,
And bryngen harneys right inough for the; 755
And ches the beste, and lef the worste for me.
And mete and drynke this night wil I brynge
Inough for the, and clothes for thy beddynge.
And if so be that thou my lady wynne,
And sle me in this woode ther I am inne, 760
Thou maist wel han thy lady as for me."
This Palamon answerde: "I graunte it the."
And thus they ben departed til a-morwe,
When ech of hem hadde leyd his feith to borwe.
    O Cupide, out of alle charité! 765
O regne, that wolt no felawe han with the!
Ful soth is seyd, that love ne lordschipe
Wol not, his thonkes, han no felaweschipe.
Wel fynden that Arcite and Palamoun.
Arcite is riden anon unto the toun, 770
And on the morwe, or it were dayes light,
Ful prively two harneys hath he dight,

---

764. *To borwe.* This expression has the same force as *to wedde*, in
    pledge. See l. 360.
768, 1249. *His thonkes*, willingly, with his good-will.

Bothe suffisaunt and mete to darreyne
The bataylle in the feeld betwix hem tweyne.
And on his hors, allone as he was born,   775
He caryeth al this harneys him byforn;
And in the grove, at tyme and place i-set,
This Arcite and this Palamon ben met.
Tho chaungen gan the colour in here face.
Right as the honter in the regne of Trace   780
That stondeth at the gappe with a spere,
Whan honted is the lyoun or the bere,
And hereth him come ruschyng in the greves,
And breketh bothe bowes and the leves,
And thinketh, "Here cometh my mortel enemy,   785
Withoute faile, he mot be deed or I;
For eyther I mot slen him at the gappe,
Or he moot sleen me, if that me myshappe:"
So ferden they, in chaungyng of here hewe,
As fer as everich of hem other knewe.   790
Ther nas no good day, ne no saluyng;
But streyt withouten word or rehersyng,
Everych of hem help for to armen other,
As frendly as he were his owne brother;
And after that with scharpe speres stronge   795
They foynen ech at other wonder longe.
Thou myghtest wene that this Palamon
In his fightynge were as a wood lyoun,
And as a cruel tygre was Arcite:
As wilde boores gonne they to smyte,   800
That frothen white as foom for ire wood.
Up to the ancle foughte they in here blood.
And in this wise I lete hem fightyng dwelle;
And forth I wol of Theseus yow telle.
    The destyné, mynistre general,   805
That executeth in the world over-al
The purveiauns, that God hath seyn byforn;
So strong it is, that though the world hadde sworn

---

807. *Hath seyn byforn*, hath seen before, hath foreseen.

The contrarye of a thing by ye or nay,
Yet somtyme it schal falle upon a day   810
That falleth nought eft withinne a thousand yeere.
For certeynly oure appetites heere,
Be it of werre, or pees, or hate, or love,
Al is it reuled by the sighte above.
This mene I now by mighty Theseus,   815
That for to honten is so desirous,
And namely at the grete hert in May,
That in his bed ther daweth him no day,
That he nys clad, and redy for to ryde
With honte and horn, and houndes him byside.   820
For in his hontyng hath he such delyt,
That it is al his joye and appetyt
To been himself the grete hertes bane,
For after Mars he serveth now Diane.
    Cleer was the day, as I have told or this,   825
And Theseus, with alle joye and blys,
With his Ypolita, the fayre queene,
And Emelye, clothed al in greene,
On honting be thay riden ryally.
And to the grove, that stood ful faste by,   830
In which ther was an hert as men him tolde,
Duk Theseus the streyte wey hath holde.
And to the launde he rydeth him ful righte,
For thider was the hert wont have his flighte,
And over a brook, and so forth in his weye.   835
This duk wol han a cours at him or tweye
With houndes, swiche as that him lust comaunde.
And whan this duk was come unto the launde.
Under the sonne he loketh, and anon
He was war of Arcite and Palamon,   840
That foughten breeme, as it were boores tuo;
The brighte swerdes wente to and fro
So hidously, that with the leste strook
It seemede as it wolde felle an ook;

---

818. *Ther daweth him no day*, no day dawns upon him.
820. *Honte* is here written for *hunte*, hunter.

But what they were, nothing he ne woot. 845
This duk his courser with his spores smoot,
And at a stert he was betwix hem tuoo,
And pullede out a swerd and cride, "Hoo!
Nomore, up peyne of leesyng of *y*oure heed.
By mighty Mars, he schal anon be deed, 850
That smyteth eny strook, that I may seen!
But telleth me what mester men *y*e been,
That ben so hardy for to fighten heere
Withoute jugge or other officere,
As it were in a lystes really?" 855
This Palamon answerde hastily,
And seyde: "Sire, what nedeth wordes mo?
We han the deth deserved bothe tuo.
Tuo woful wrecches been we, tuo kaytyves,
That ben encombred of oure owne lyves; 860
And as thou art a rightful lord and juge,
Ne *y*eve us neyther mercy ne refuge.
And sle me first, for seynte charité;
But sle my felawe eek as wel as me.
Or sle him first; for, though thou knowe it lyte, 865
This is thy mortal fo, this is Arcite,
That fro thy lond is banyscht on his heed,
For which he hath deserved to be deed.
For this is he that com unto thi gate
And seyde, that he highte Philostrate. 870
Thus hath he japed the ful many a *y*er,
And thou hast maked him thy cheef squyer.
And this is he that loveth Emelye.
For sith the day is come that I schal dye,
I make pleynly my confessioun, 875
That I am thilke woful Palamoun,
That hath thy prisoun broke wikkedly.
I am thy mortal foo, and it am I

---

848. *Hoo*, an exclamation made by heralds, to stop the fight. It was
  also used to enjoin silence. See ll. 1675, 1798.
878. *It am I.* This is the regular construction in early English. In
  modern English the pronoun *it* is regarded as the direct nominative, and *I* as forming part of the predicate.

That loveth so hoote Emelye the brighte,
That I wol dye present in hire sighte. 880
Therefore I aske deeth and my juwyse;
But slee my felawe in the same wyse,
For bothe han we deserved to be slayn."
    This worthy duk answerde anon agayn,
And seide, " This is a schort conclusioun: 885
Youre owne mouthe, by youre confessioun,
Hath dampned you, and I wil it recorde.
It nedeth nought to pyne yow with the corde.
Ye schul be deed by mighty Mars the reede!"
The queen anon for verray wommanhede 890
Gan for to wepe, and so dede Emelye,
And alle the ladies in the companye.
Gret pité was it, as it thoughte hem alle,
That evere such a chaunce schulde falle;
For gentil men thei were, of gret estate, 895
And nothing but for love was this debate.
And sawe here bloody woundes wyde and sore;
And alle cryden, bothe lasse and more,
"Have mercy, Lord, upon us wommen alle!"
And on here bare knees adoun they falle, 900
And wolde han kist his feet ther as he stood,
Til atte laste aslaked was his mood;
For pité renneth sone in gentil herte.
And though he first for ire quok and sterte,
He hath considerd shortly in a clause, 905
The trespas of hem bothe, and eek the cause:
And although that his ire here gylt accusede,
Yet in his resoun he hem bothe excusede;
And thus he thoughte wel that every man
Wol helpe himself in love if that he can, 910
And eek delyvere himself out of prisoun;
And eek his herte hadde compassioun

---

881. Therefore I ask my death and my doom.
889. *Mars the reede.*—Boccaccio uses the same epithet in the opening of
    his Teseide; " *O rubiconde Marte.*" *Reede* refers to the color of
    the planet.
903. This line occurs again, Squire's Tale, ii. 133.

Of wommen, for they wepen evere in oon;
And in his gentil herte he thoughte anoon,
And softe unto himself he seyde: "Fy   915
Upon a lord that wol han no mercy,
But ben a lyoun bothe in word and dede,
To hem that ben in repentaunce and drede,
As wel as to a proud despitous man,
That wol maynteyne that he first bigan!   920
That lord hath litel of discrecioun,
That in such caas can no divisioun;
But weyeth pride and humblesse after oon."
And schortly, whan his ire is thus agon,
He gan to loken up with eyen lighte,   925
And spak these same wordes al on highte.
"The god of love, a! *benedicite*,
How mighty and how gret a lord is he!
Agayns his might ther gayneth non obstacles,
He may be cleped a god for his miracles;   930
For he can maken at his own gyse
Of everych herte, as that him lust devyse.
Lo her this Arcite and this Palamoun,
That quytly weren out of my prisoun,
And mighte han lyved in Thebes ryally,   935
And witen I am here mortal enemy,
And that here deth lith in my might also,
And *y*et hath love, maugre here ey*gh*en tuo,
I-brought hem hider bothe for to dye.
Now loketh, is nat that an heih folye?   940
Who may not ben a fool, if that he love?
Byhold for Goddes sake that sit above,

---

922. *Can no divisoun*, knows no distinction.
923. *After oon = after one mode*, according to the same rule.
925. *Eyen lighte*, cheerful looks.
941. "Amare et Sapere vix Deo conceditur." (Pub. Sent. 15.) Cp. Adv.
    of Learning, ii. proem. § 15. "It is impossible to love and to be
    wise." (Bacon's Essays, ed. Singer. x. p. 34.)
    Not (Harl.); omitted by Elles, which has *Who may been a fole
    but-if he love,*

Se how they blede! be they nought wel arrayed?
Thus hath here lord, the god of love, y-payed
Here wages and here fees for here servise. 945
And yet they wenen for to ben ful wise
That serven love, for ought that may bifalle.
But this is yet the beste game of alle,
That sche, for whom they han this jolitee,
Can hem therfore as moche thank as me. 950
Sche woot no more of al this hoote fare,
By God, than wot a cockow or an hare.
But al moot ben assayed, hoot and cold;
A man moot ben a fool or yong or old;
I woot it by myself ful yore agon: 955
For in my tyme a servant was I on.
And therfore, syn I knowe of loves peyne,
And wot how sore it can a man distreyne,
As he that hath ben caught ofte in his laas,
I you foryeve al holly this trespaas, 960
At requeste of the queen that kneleth heere,
And eek of Emelye, my suster deere.
And ye schul bothe anon unto me swere,
That neveremo ye schul my corowne dere,
Ne make werre upon me night ne day, 965
But ben my freendes in al that ye may.
I yow foryeve this trespas every del."
And they him swore his axyng fayre and wel,
And him of lordschipe and of mercy prayde,
And he hem graunteth grace, and thus he sayde: 970
" To speke of real lynage and richesse,
Though that sche were a queen or a pryncesse,
Ech of yow bothe is worthy douteles
To wedden when tyme is, but natheles
I speke as for my suster Emelye, 975
For whom ye han this stryf and jelousye,
Ye wite youreself sche may not wedde two
At oones, though ye fighten evere mo:

949. *Jolitee*, joyfulness—said of course ironically.
950. *Can. ... thank*, acknowledges an obligation, owes thanks.

That oon of *y*ow, al be him loth or leef,

He mot go pypen in an ivy leef;   980

This is to sayn, sche may nought now han bothe,

Al be *y*e nevere so jelous, ne so wrothe.

And for-thy I *y*ou putte in this degré,

That ech of *y*ou schal have his destyné,

As him is schape, and herkneth in what wyse;   985

Lo here *y*oure ende of that I schal devyse.

   My wil is this, for plat conclusioun,

Withouten eny repplicacioun,

If that *y*ou liketh, tak it for the beste,

That everych of *y*ou schal gon wher him leste   990

Frely withouten raunsoun or daunger;

And this day fyfty wykes, fer ne neer,

---

979. *Loth* or *leef*, displeasing or pleasing.

980. *Pypen in an ivy leef* is an expression like " blow the buck's-horn,"
to console oneself with any useless or frivolous employment; it
occurs again in Troilus, v. 1434. Cp. the expression "to go and
whistle."

992. *Fer ne neer*, farther nor nearer, neither more nor less. "After
some little trouble, I have arrived at the conclusion that Chaucer ·
has given us sufficient *data* for ascertaining both the days of the
month and of the week of many of the principal events of the
'Knightes Tale.' The following scheme will explain many things
hitherto unnoticed.

   "On Friday, May 4, before 1 A.M., Palamon breaks out of prison.
For (1. 605) it was during the 'third night of May, but (1. 609) a little
after midnight.' That it was Friday is evident also, from observ-
ing that Palamon hides himself at day's approach, whilst Arcite
rises 'for to doon his observance to May, remembryng of the
poynt of his desire.' To do this best, he would go into the fields
at *sunrise* (1. 633), during the hour dedicated to *Venus*, i. e. during
the hour after sunrise *on a Friday.*

   "We must understand ' Fyfty wekes' to be a poetical expression
for a *year*. This is not mere supposition, however, but a *certainty;*
because the appointed day was in the month of *May*, whereas fifty
weeks and no more would land us in *April*. Then 'this day fyfty
wekes' means ' this day year,' viz. on May 5.

   "Now, in the year following (supposed not a leap-year), the 5th
of May would be *Sunday*. But this we are expressly told in l. 1330.
It must be noted, however, that this is not the day of the *tournament*, but of the *muster* for it, as may be gleaned from ll. 992-995

Everich of *y*ou schal brynge an hundred knightes,
Armed for lystes up at alle rightes,
Al redy to derrayne hire by bataylle.   995
And this byhote I *y*ou withouten fa*y*lle
Upon my trouthe, and as I am a knight,
That whether of *y*ow bothe that hath might,
This is to seyn, that whether he or thou
May with his hundred, as I spak of now,   1000
Slen his contrarye, or out of lystes dryve,
Thanne schal I *y*even Emelye to wyve,
To whom that fortune *y*eveth so fair a grace.
The lystes schal I maken in this place,
And God so wisly on my sowle rewe,   1005
As I schal evene juge ben and trewe.
*Y*e schul non other ende with me make,
That oon of *y*ow ne schal be deed or take.
And if *y*ou thinketh this is wel i-sayd,
Sayeth *y*oure avys, and holdeth *y*ow apayd.   1010
This is *y*oure ende and *y*oure conclusioun."
Who loketh lightly now but Palamoun?
Who spryngeth up for joye but Arcite?
Who couthe telle, or who couthe it endite,

---

and 1238. The tenth hour 'inequal' of Sunday night, or the second
hour before sunrise of Monday, is dedicated to *Venus*, as explained
by Tyrwhitt (1. 1359); and therefore Palamon then goes to the temple of Venus. The third ·hour after this, the first after sunrise on Monday, is dedicated to Luna or Diana, and during this
Emily goes to Diana's temple. The third hour after this again,
the fourth after sunrise, is dedicated to Mars, and therefore Arcite
then goes to the temple of Mars. But the rest of the day is spent
merely in jousting and preparations—
      "' Al the *Monday* jousten they and daunce.' (1. 1628.)
   The tournament therefore takes place on Tuesday, May 7, on the
day of the week presided over by *Mars*, as was very fitting; and
this perhaps helps to explain Saturn's exclamation in 1. 1811,
'Mars hath his wille.'
   "Thus far all the principal days, with their events, are ex-
actly accounted for." (Walter W. Skeat.)
1008. That one of you shall be either slain or taken prisoner, i. e. one of
   you must be fairly conquered.

The joye that is maked in the place   1015
Whan Theseus hath don so fair a grace?
But down on knees wente every maner wight,
And thanken him with al here herte and miht,
And namely the Thebans ofte sithe.
And thus with good hope and with herte blithe   1020
They take here leve, and hom-ward gonne they ryde
To Thebes with his olde walles wyde.
  I trowe men wolde deme it necligence,
If I foryete to telle the dispence
Of Theseus, that goth so busily   1025
To maken up the lystes rially;
That such a noble theatre as it was,
I dar wel sayn that in this world ther nas.
The circuit a myle was aboute,
Walled of stoon, and dyched al withoute.   1030
Round was the schap, in manere of compaas,
Ful of degrees, the heighte of sixty paas
That whan a man was set on o degré
He lette nought his felawe for to se.
  Est-ward ther stood a gate of marbel whit,   1035
West-ward right such another in the opposit.
And schortly to conclude, such a place
Was non in erthe as in so litel space;
For in the lond ther nas no crafty man,
That geometrye or arsmetrike can,   1040
Ne portreyour, ne kervere of ymages,
That Theseus ne yaf hem mete and wages
The theatre for to maken and devyse.
And for to don his ryte and sacrifise,
He est-ward hath upon the gate above,   1045
In worschipe of Venus, goddesse of love,

1031. The various parts of this round theatre are subsequently described. On the North was the turret of Diana with oratory; on
the East the gate of Venus with altar above; on the West the temple of Mars, with Northern door, very narrow (l. 1126), through
which the light shone in (l. 1129).

1032. *Ful of degrees*, full of steps (placed one above another, as in an
amphitheatre).

Don make an auter and an oratorye;
And west-ward, in the mynde and in memorye
Of Mars, he hath i-maked such another,
That coste largely of gold a fother, 1050
And north-ward, in a toret on the walle,
Of alabaster whit and reed coralle
An oratorye riche for to see,
In worschipe of Dyane, of chastité,
Hath Theseus doon wrought in noble wise. 1055
But yit hadde I foryeten to devyse
The noble kervyng, and the purtreitures,
The schap, the contenaunce and the figures,
That weren in these oratories thre.
First in the temple of Venus maystow se 1060
Wrought on the wal, ful pitous to byholde,
The broken slepes, and the sykes colde;
The sacred teeres, and the waymentyng;
The fyry strokes of the desiryng,
That loves servauntz in this lyf enduren; 1065
The othes, that here covenantz assuren.
Plesaunce and hope, desyr, fool-hardynesse,
Beauté and youthe, bauderye and richesse,
Charmes and force, lesynges and flaterye,
Dispense, busynesse, and jelousye, 1070
That werede of yelwe guldes a gerland,
And a cokkow sittyng on hire hand;
Festes, instrumentz, caroles, daunces,
Lust and array, and alle the circumstaunces
Of love, whiche that I rekned have and schal, 1075
By ordre weren peynted on the wal.
And mo than I can make of mencioun.
For sothly al the mount of Citheroun,

1048. *And on the* westward [side] in memorie.
1061. *On the wal,* viz. over the gate and wall, i. e. over a sort of bar-
bican.
1071. *Guldes.* a *gold* or turnsol. The corn - marigold in the North is
called *goulans, guilde,* or *goles.* and in the South, *golds.*
1078. *Citheroun = Cithaeron,* sacred to Venus.

Ther Venus hath hire principal dwellyng,
Was schewed on the wall in portreying,   1080
With al the gardyn, and the lustynesse.
Nought was foryete the porter Ydelnesse,
Ne Narcisus the fayre of yore agon,
Ne yet the folye of kyng Salamon,
Ne eek the grete strengthe of Hercules,   1085
Thenchauntementz of Medea and Circes,
Ne of Turnus with the hardy fiers corage,
The riche Cresus caytif in servage.
Thus may ye seen that wisdom ne richesse,
Beauté ne sleighte, strengthe, ne hardynesse,   1090
Ne may with Venus holde champartye,
For as hire lust the world than may sche gye,
Lo, alle thise folk i-caught were in hire las,
Til they for wo ful often sayde allas.
Sufficeth heere ensamples oon or tuo,   1095
And though I couthe rekne a thousend mo.
The statue of Venus, glorious for to see,
Was naked fletyng in the large see,
And fro the navele doun al covered was
With wawes grene, and brighte as eny glas.   1100
A citole in hire right hond hadde sche,
And on hire heed, ful semely for to see,
A rose garland fresch and wel smellyng,
Above hire heed hire dowves flikeryng.
Biforn hire stood hire some Cupido,   1105
Upon his schuldres wynges hadde he two;
And blynd he was, as it is ofte seene;
A bowe he bar and arwes brighte and kene.
Why schulde I nought as wel eek telle you al
The portreiture, that was upon the wal   1110
Withinne the temple of mighty Mars the reede?
Al peynted was the wal in lengthe and breede

1082. In the Romaunt of the Rose, *Idleness* is the *porter* of the garden in
    which the rose (Beauty) is kept.
1083. *Of yore agon*, of years gone by.

Lik to the estres of the grisly place,
That highte the grete temple of Mars in Trace,
In thilke colde frosty regioun,   1115
Ther as Mars hath his sovereyn mancioun.
First on the wal was peynted a forest,
In which ther dwelleth neyther man ne best,
With knotty knarry bareyne trees olde
Of stubbes scharpe and hidous to byholde;   1120
In which ther ran a swymbel in a swough,
As though a storm schulde bersten every bough:
And downward on an hil under a bente,
Ther stood the temple of Marz armypotente,
Wrought al of burned steel, of which thentré   1125
Was long and streyt, and gastly for to see.
And therout cam a rage and such a vese,
That it made all the gates for to rese.
The northen light in at the dores schon,
For wyndowe on the wal ne was ther noon,   1130

1121. *A swymbel in a swough,* a moaning (or sighing) in a general com-
    motion (caused by the wind).

1124. *Marz armypotente.*
      "O thou rede Marz armypotente,
        That in the trende baye hase made thy throne;
        That God arte of bataile and regent,
        And rulest all that alone;
        To whom I profre precious present,
        To the makande my moone
        With herte, body and alle myn entente,

      .   .   .   .   .

        In worshippe of thy reverence
        On thyn owen Tewesdaye."
                            (Sowdone of Babyloyne, p. 35.)

1127. *Vese* is glossed *impetus* in the Ellesmere MS.   Mr. Skeat once sug-
    gested that it is the *bise* or North wind (the *North* belongs to Mars
    in l. 1129); but now thinks the above gloss to be right.   See the
    Glossary.

1128. *Rese* = to shake, quake.

1129. "I suppose the *northern light* is the aurora borealis, but this phe-
    nomenon is so rarely mentioned by mediæval writers, that it may
    be questioned whether Chaucer meant anything more than the
    faint and cold illumination received by reflexion through the door
    of an apartment fronting the north." (Marsh.)

Thurgh which men mighten any light discerne.
The dores were alle of ademauntz eterne,
I-clenched overthwart and endelong
With iren tough; and, for to make it strong,
Every piler the temple to susteene   1135
Was tonne greet, of iren bright and schene.
Ther saugh I first the derke ymaginyng
Of felonye, and al the compassyng;
The cruel ire, as reed as eny gleede;
The pikepurs, and eek the pale drede;   1140
The smylere with the knyf under the cloke;
The schepne brennyng with the blake smoke;
The tresoun of the murtheryng in the bed;
The open werre, with woundes al bi-bled;
Contek with bloody knyf, and scharp manace.   1145
Al ful of chirkyng was that sory place.
The sleere of himself yet saugh I there,
His herte-blood hath bathed al his here;
The nayl y-dryven in the schode a-nyght;
The colde deth, with mouth gapyng upright.   1150
Amyddes of the temple sat meschaunce,
With disconfort and sory contenaunce.
Yet saugh I woodnesse laughying in his rage;
Armed complaint, outhees, and fiers outrage.
The caroigne in the bussh, with throte y-corve: 1155
A thousand slain, and not of qualme y-storve;
The tiraunt, with the prey by force y-raft;
The toun destroied, ther was no thyng laft.
Yet sawgh I brent the schippes hoppesteres;
The hunte strangled with the wilde beres: 1160
The sowe freten the child right in the cradel;
The cook i-skalded, for al his longe ladel.

1146. *Chirkyng* is properly the cry of birds.
1149. This line contains an allusion to the death of Sisera, Judges iv.
1159. *Hoppesteres.*—Speght explains this word by pilots (*gubernaculum tenentes*). Others explain it *hopposteres = opposteres =* opposing, hostile, so that *schippes hoppesteres = bellatrices carinœ* (Statius.)
1162. *For al,* notwithstanding.

Nought was for*y*eten by the infortune of Marte;
The cartere over-ryden with his carte,
Under the whel ful lowe he lay adoun.   1165
Ther were also of Martes divisioun,
The barbour, and the bocher; and the smyth
That forgeth scharpe swerdes on his stith.
And al above depeynted in a tour
Saw I conquest sittyng in gret honour,   1170
With the scharpe swerd over his heed
Haugynge by a sotil twynes threed.
Depeynted was the slaughtre of Julius,
Of grete Nero, and of Anthonius;
Al be that thilke tyme they were unborn,   1175
*Y*et was here deth depeynted ther byforn,
By manasyng of Mars, right by figure,
So was it schewed in that purtreiture
As is depeynted in the sterres above,
Who schal be slayn or elles deed for love.   1180
Sufficeth oon ensample in stories olde,
I may not rekne hem alle, though I wolde.
    The statue of Mars upon a carte stood,
Armed, and lokede grym as he were wood;

1163. *Infortune of Marte.* Tyrwhitt thinks that Chaucer might intend to
    be satirical in these lines; but the introduction of such apparently
    undignified incidents arose from the confusion already mentioned
    of the god of war with the planet to which his name was given,
    and the influence of which was supposed to produce all the disasters
    here mentioned. The following extract from the Compost of Ptole-
    meus gives some of the supposed effect of Mars: "Under Mars is
    borne theves and robbers that kepe hye wayes, and do hurte to
    true men, and nyght walkers, and quarell pykers, bosters, mock-
    ers, and skoffers, and these men of Mars causeth warre and mur-
    ther, and batayle, they wyll be gladly *smythes* or workers of yron,
    lyght fyngred, and lyers, gret swerers of othes in vengeable wyse,
    and a great summyler and crafty. He is red and angry, with
    blacke heer and lytell iyen; he shall be a great walker, and a
    maker of swordes and knyves, and a sheder of mannes blode, and
    a fornycatour, and a speker of rybawdry . . . and good to be a
    barboure and a blode letter, and to draw tethe, and is peryllous of
    his handes."

And over his heed ther schynen two figures   1185
Of sterres, that been cleped in scriptures,
That oon Puella, that other Rubeus.
This god of armes was arrayed thus:—
A wolf ther stood byforn him at his feet
With eyen reede, and of a man he eet;   1190
With sotyl pencel depeynted was this storie,
In redoutyng of Mars and of his glorie.
   Now to the temple of Dyane the chaste
As schortly as I can I wol me haste,
To telle *y*ou al the descripcioun.   1195
Depeynted ben the walles up and down,
Of huntyng and of schamefast chastité.
Ther saugh I how woful Calystopé,
Whan that Dyane agreved was with here,
Was turned from a womman to a bere,   1200
And after was sche maad the loode-sterre;
Thus was it peynted, I can say you no ferre;
Hire sone is eek a sterre, as men may see.
Ther sawgh I Dane yturned til a tree,
I mene nou*gh*t the goddesse Dyane,   1205
But Penneus dou*gh*ter, which that highte Dane.
Ther saugh I Atheon an hert i-maked,
For vengeaunce that he saugh Dyane al naked;

1187. The names of two figures in geomancy, representing two constellations in heaven. " Puella signifieth Mars retrograde, and Rubeus Mars direct." (Speght.)

1198. *Calystopé* = *Callisto*, a daughter of Lycaon, King of Arcadia, and companion of Diana.

1201, 1203. " Cp. Ovid's Fasti, ii. 153–192; especially 189, 190,
    'Signa propinqua micant. Prior est, quam dicimus Arcton,
    Arctophylax formam terga sequentis habet.' "
The nymph Callisto was changed into *Arctos* or the Great Bear. This was sometimes confused with the other 'Arctos or Lesser Bear, in which was situate the *lodestar* or Polestar. Chaucer has followed this error.

1204, 1206. *Dane* = *Daphne*, a girl beloved by Apollo, and changed into a laurel. See Berens's Mythology.

1207. *Atheon* = *Actaeon*. See Berens's Mythology.

I saugh how that his houndes han him caught,
And freten him, for that they knewe him naught. 1210
Yit peynted was a litel forthermoor,
How Atthalaunte huntede the wilde boor,
And Meleagre, and many another mo,
For which Dyane wroughte hem care and woo.
Ther saugh I many another wonder storye, 1215
The whiche me list not drawe to memorye.
This goddesse on an hert ful hyhe seet,
With smale hounds al aboute hire feet,
And undernethe hire feet sche hadde a moone,
Wexyng it was, and schulde wane soone. 1220
In gaude greene hire statue clothed was,
With bowe in honde, and arwes in a cas.
Hir eyghen caste sche ful lowe adoun,
Ther Pluto hath his derke regioun.
A womman travailyng was hire biforn, 1225
But, for hire child so longe was unborn,
Ful pitously Lucyna gan sche calle,
And seyde, "Help, for thou mayst best of alle."
Wel couthe he peynte lyfly that it wroughte,
With many a floryn he the hewes boughte. 1230
    Now been thise listes maad, and Theseus
That at his grete cost arrayede thus
The temples and the theatre every del,
Whan it was don, hym likede wonder wel.
But stynte I wil of Theseus a lite, 1235
And speke of Palamon and of Arcite.
    The day approcheth of here retournynge,
That everych schulde an hundred knightes brynge,
The bataille to derreyne, as I you tolde;
And til Athenes, here covenant to holde, 1240
Hath everych of hem brought an hundred knightes
Wel armed for the werre at alle rightes.

1212. *Atthalaunte* = *Atalanta*. See Berens's Mythology.
1216. *Not drawe to memorye* = *not drawen to memory*, not call to mind.
1228. *Thou mayst best*, art best able to help, thou hast most power.

And sikerly ther trowede many a man
That nevere, siththen that the world bigan,
As for to speke of knighthod of here hond,　　　　1245
As fer as God hath maked see or lond,
Nas, of so fewe, so noble a companye.
For every wight that lovede chyvalrye,
And wolde, his thankes, han a passant name,
Hath preyed that he mighte ben of that game;　　　　1250
And wel was him, that therto chosen was.
For if ther felle to morwe such a caas,
Ye knowen wel, that every lusty knight,
That loveth paramours, and hath his might,
Were it in Engelond, or elleswhere,　　　　1255
They wolde, here thankes, wilne to be there.
To fighte for a lady; *benedicite !*
It were a lusty sighte for to see.
And right so ferden they with Palamon.
With him ther wente knyghtes many oon;　　　　1260
Som wol ben armed in an habergoun,
In a brest-plat and in a light gypoun;
And somme woln have a peyre plates large;
And somme woln have a Pruce scheld, or a targe;
Somme woln been armed on here legges weel,　　　　1265
And have an ax, and somme a mace of steel.
Ther nys no newe gyse, that it nas old.
Armed were they, as I have you told,
Everich after his opinioun.

　　Ther maistow sen comyng with Palamoun　　　　1270
Ligurge himself, the grete kyng of Trace;
Blak was his berd, and manly was his face.
The cercles of his eyen in his heed
They gloweden bytwixe *y*elwe and reed;
And lik a griffoun lokede he aboute,　　　　1275
With kempe heres on his browes stowte;

1257. *Benedicite* is pronounced nearly as a trisyllable. It *is* so sometimes, though five syllables in l 927.
1267. This line seems to mean that there is nothing new under the sun.
1276. *Kempe heres*, shaggy, rough hairs. Tyrwhitt and subsequent edi-

His lymes greete, his brawnes harde and stronge,
His schuldres broode, his armes rounde and longe.
And as the gyse was in his contré,
Ful heye upon a char of gold stood he, 1280
With foure white boles in the trays.
Instede of cote-armure over his harnays,
With nayles yelwe, and brighte as eny gold,
He hadde a beres skyn, col-blak, for-old.
His longe heer was kembd byhynde his bak, 1285
As eny ravenes fether it schon for-blak.
A wrethe of gold arm-gret, of huge wighte,
Upon his heed, set ful of stoones brighte,
Of fyne rubies and of dyamauntz.
Aboute his char ther wenten white alauntz, 1290
Twenty and mo, as grete as eny steer,
To hunten at the lyoun or the deer,
And folwede him, with mosel faste i-bounde,
Colers of golde, and torettz fyled rounde.
An hundred lordes hadde he in his route 1295
Armed ful wel, with hertes sterne and stoute.
    With Arcita, in stories as men fynde,
The grete Emetreus, the kyng of Ynde,
Uppon a steede bay, trapped in steel,
Covered in cloth of gold dyapred wel, 1300
Cam rydyng lyk the god of armes, Mars.
His coote-armure was of cloth of Tars,
Cowched with perles whyte and rounde and grete.
His sadel was of brend gold newe ybete;

---

tors have taken for granted that *kempe = kemped*, combed; but *kempe* is rather the reverse of this, and instead of smoothly combed, means bent, *curled*, and hence rough, shaggy.

1284. *For-old*, very old.

1286. *For-blak* is generally explained as *for blackness;* it means *very black*.

1294. *Colers of*, having collars of. Some MSS. read *colerd with*.
    Torettz, probably rings that will turn round, because they pass through an eye which is a little larger than the thickness of the ring. (Skeat.)

1302. *Cloth of Tars*, a kind of silk, said to be the same as in other places is called *Tartarine*.

A mantelet upon his schuldre hangynge 　　　　1305
Bret-ful of rubies reede, as fir sparklynge.
His crispe heer lik rynges was i-ronne,
And that was yelwe, and gliterede as the sonne.
His nose was heigh, his eyen bright cytryn,
His lippes rounde, his colour was sangwyn, 　　1310
A fewe fraknes in his face y-spreynd,
Betwixen yelwe and somdel blak y-meynd,
And as a lyoun he his lokyng caste.
Of fyve and twenty yeer his age I caste.
His berd was wel bygonne for to sprynge; 　　1315
His voys was as a trumpe thunderynge.
Upon his heed he werede of laurer grene
A garlond fresch and lusty for to sene.
Upon his hond he bar for his deduyt
An egle tame, as eny lylie whyt. 　　　　　　1320
An hundred lordes hadde he with him ther,
Al armed sauf here hedes in here ger,
Ful richely in alle maner thinges.
For trusteth wel, that dukes, erles, kynges,
Were gadred in this noble compainye, 　　　　1325
For love, and for encrees of chivalrye.
Aboute this kyng ther ran on every part
Ful many a tame lyoun and lepart.
And in this wise thise lordes alle and some
Been on the Sonday to the cité come 　　　　1330
Aboute prime, and in the toun alight.
This Theseus, this duk, this worthy knight,
Whan he hadde brought hem into his cité,
And ynned hem, everich at his degré
He festeth him, and doth so gret labour 　　　1335
To esen hem, and don hem al honour,
That yit men wene that no mannes wyt
Of non estat ne cowde amenden it.
The mynstralcye, the servyce at the feste,
The grete yiftes to the moste and leste, 　　　1340

1329. *Alle and some*, "all and singular," "one and all."

The riche array of Theseus paleys,
Ne who sat first ne last upon the deys,
What ladies fayrest ben or best daunsynge,
Or which of hem can daunce best and singe,
Ne who most felyngly speketh of love;   1345
What haukes sitten on the perche above,
What houndes liggen on the floor adoun:
Of al this make I now no mencioun,
But of theffect; that thinketh me the beste;
Now comth the poynt, and herkneth if *y*ou leste. 1350
   The Sonday night, or day bigan to springe,
When Palamon the larke herde synge,
Although it nere nought day by houres tuo,
*Y*it sang the larke, and Palamon also.
With holy herte, and with an heih corage   1355
He roos, to wenden on his pilgrymage
Unto the blisful Citherea benigne,
I mene Venus, honurable and digne.
And in hire hour he walketh forth a paas

1359. *And in hire hour.* The first hour of the Sunday, reckoning from
sunrise, belonged to the sun, the planet of the day; the second to
Venus, the third to Mercury, &c.; and continuing this method of
allotment, we shall find that the twenty-second hour also belonged
to the Sun, and the twenty-third to Venus; so that the hour of
Venus really was, as Chaucer says, two hours before the sunrise
of the following day. Accordingly, we are told in l. 1413, that the
third hour after Palamon set out for the temple of Venus, the Sun
rose, and Emily began to go to the temple of Diane. It is not said
that this was the hour of Diane, or the Moon, but it really was: for,
as we have just seen, the twenty-third hour of Sunday belonged to
Venus, the twenty-fourth must be given to Mercury, and the first
hour of Monday falls in course to the Moon, the presiding planet
of that day. After this Arcite is described as walking to the temple of Mars, l. 1509, in *the nexte houre of Mars*, that is, the *fourth*
hour of the day. It is necessary to take these words together, for
the nexte houre, singly, would signify the *second* hour of the day;
but that, according to the rule of rotation mentioned above,
belonged to Saturn, as the *third* did to Jupiter. The *fourth* was
the nexte houre of Mars that occurred after the hour last named.
(Tyrwhitt.) In fact, just as Emily is three hours later than Palamon, so Arcite is three hours later than Emily. (Skeat.)

Unto the lystes, ther hire temple was, 1360
And doun he kneleth, and, with humble cheere
And herte sore, he seide as ye schul heere.
"Faireste of faire, o lady myn Venus,
Doughter of Jove, and spouse to Vulcanus,
Thou gladere of the mount of Citheroun, 1365
For thilke love thou haddest to Adoun
Have pité of my bittre teeres smerte,
Aud tak myn humble prayere to thin herte.
Allas! I ne have no langage to telle
Theffectes ne the tormentz of myn helle; 1370
Myn herte may myne harmes nat bewreye;
I am so confus, that I cannot seye.
But mercy, lady brighte, that knowest wele
My thought, and seest what harmes that I fele,
Considre al this, and rewe upon my sore, 1375
As wisly as I schal for evermore,
Emforth my might, thi trewe servaunt be,
And holden werre alway with chastité;
That make I myn avow, so ye me helpe.
I kepe nat of armes for to yelpe. 1380
Ne I ne aske nat to-morwe to have victorie,
Ne renoun in this caas, ne veyne glorie
Of pris of armes, blowen up and doun,
But I wolde have fully possessioun
Of Emelye, and dye in thi servise; 1385
Fynd thou the manere how, and in what wyse
I recche nat, but it may better be,
To have victorie of hem, or they of me,
So that I have my lady in myne armes.
For though so be that Mars is god of armes, 1390
Youre vertu is so gret in hevene above,
That if you list I schal wel han my love.
Thy temple wol I worschipe everemo,

1366. *Adoun*, Adonis.
1380. I care not of arms (success in arms) to boast.
1381. *Ne I ne aske* &c., are to be pronounced as *ni naske*, &c. So in l.
    1772 of this tale, *Ne in* must be pronounced as *nin*.

And on thin auter, wher I ryde or go,
I wol don sacrifice, and fyres beete.   1395
And if ye wol nat so, my lady sweete,
Than praye I the, to-morwe with a spere
That Arcita me thurgh the herte bere.
Thanne rekke I nat, whan I have lost my lyf,
Though that Arcite wynne hire to his wyf.   1400
This is theffect and ende of my prayere,
Yif me my love, thou blisful lady deere."
Whan thorisoun was doon of Palamon,
His sacrifice he dede, and that anoon
Ful pitously, with alle circumstaunces,   1405
Al telle I nat as now his observaunces.
But atte laste the statue of Venus schook,
And made a signe, wherby that he took
That his prayere accepted was that day.
For though the signe schewede a delay,   1410
Yet wiste he wel that graunted was his boone;
And with glad herte he wente him hom ful soone.
    The thridde hour inequal that Palamon
Bigan to Venus temple for to goon,
Up roose the sonne, and up roos Emelye,   1415
And to the temple of Diane gan sche hye.
Hire maydens, that sche thider with hire ladde,
Ful redily with hem the fyr they hadde,
Thencens, the clothes, and the remenant al
That to the sacrifice longen schal;   1420
The hornes fulle of meth, as was the gyse;
Ther lakkede nought to don hire sacrifise.
Smokyng the temple, ful of clothes faire,

1394. *Wher I ryde or go*, whether I ride or walk.
1395. *Fyres beete*, to kindle or light fires. *Beete* also signifies to mend
     or make up the fire; see l. 1434.
1413. *The thridde hour inequal.* In the astrological system, the day,
     from sunrise to sunset, and the night, from sunset to sunrise, being
     each divided into twelve hours, it is plain that the hours of the day
     and night were never equal except just at the equinoxes. The
     hours attributed to the planets were of this *unequal* sort.

This Emelye with herte debonaire
Hire body wessch with water of a welle;   1425
But how sche dide hire rite I dar nat telle,
But it be eny thing in general;
And yet it were a game to heren al;
To him that meneth wel it were no charge:
But it is good a man ben at his large.   1430
Hire brighte heer was kempt, untressed al;
A coroune of a greene ok cerial
Upon hire heed was set ful faire and meete.
Tuo fyres on the auter gan sche beete, ·
And dide hire thinges, as men may biholde   1435
In Stace of Thebes, and thise bokes olde.
Whan kyndled was the fyr, with pitous cheere
Unto Dyane sche spak, as ye may heere.
    " O chaste goddesse of the woodes greene,
To whom bothe hevene and erthe and see is seene, 1440
Queen of the regne of Pluto derk and lowe,
Goddesse of maydens, that myn herte hast knowe
Ful many a year, and woost what I desire,
As keep me fro thi vengeaunce and thin yre,
That Atheon aboughte trewely: 1445
Chaste goddesse, wel wost thou that I
Desire to ben a mayden al my lyf,
Ne nevere wol I be no love ne wyf.
I am, thou wost, yit of thi compainye,
A mayde, and love huntyng and venerye,   1450
And for to walken in the woodes wylde, `
And nought to ben a wyf, and ben with chylde.
Nought wol I knowe the compainye of man.
Now helpe me, lady, syth ye may and kan,
For tho thre formes that thou hast in the.   1455
And Palamon, that hath such love to me,

1428. *A game*, a pleasure.
1436. *In Stace of Thebes*, in the Thebaid of Statius.
1445. *Aboughte*, atoned for. Cp. the phrase " to *buy* dearly."
1455. *Thre formes*. Diana is called *Diva Triformis;*—in heaven, Luna;
    on earth, Diana and Lucina, and in hell, Proserpina.

And eek Arcite, thou loveth me so sore,
This grace I praye the withouten more,
As sende love and pees betwixe hem two;
And fro me torne awey here hertes so, 1460
That al here hoote love, and here desir,
And al here bisy torment, and here fyr
Be queynt, or turned in another place;
And if so be thou wolt do me no grace,
Or if my destyné be schapen so, 1465
That I schal needes have on of hem two,
As sende me him that most desireth me.
Bihold, goddesse of clene chastité,
The bittre teeres that on my cheekes falle.
Syn thou art mayde, and kepere of us alle, 1470
My maydenhode thou kepe and wel conserve,
And whil I lyve a mayde I wil the serve."
    The fyres brenne upon the auter cleere,
Whil Emelye was thus in hire preyere;
But sodeinly sche saugh a sighte queynte, 1475
For right anon on of the fyres queynte,
And quykede agayn, and after that anon
That other fyr was queynt, and al agon;
And as it queynte, it made a whistelynge,
As doth a wete brond in his brennynge. 1480
And at the brondes ende out-ran anoon
As it were bloody dropes many oon;
For which so sore agast was Emelye,
That sche was wel neih mad, and gan to crie,
For sche ne wiste what it signifyede; 1485
But oonly for the feere thus sche cryede
And wep, that it was pité for to heere.
And therwithal Dyane gan appeare,
With bowe in hond, right as an hunteresse,
And seyde: "Doughter, stynt thyn hevynesse. 1490
Among the goddes hye it is affermed,
And by eterne word write and confermed,
Thou schalt ben wedded unto con of tho
That han for the so moche care and wo;

But unto which of hem I may nat telle. 1495
Farwel, for I ne may no lenger dwelle.
The fyres which that on myn auter brenne
Schuln the declaren, or that thou go henne,
Thyn aventure of love, as in this caas."
And with that word, the arwes in the caas 1500
Of the goddesse clatren faste and rynge,
And forth sche wente, and made a vanysschynge,
For which this Emelye astoned was,
And seide, "What amounteth this, allas!
I putte me in thy proteccioun, 1505
Dyane, and in thi disposicioun."
And hoom sche goth anon the nexte waye.
This is theffect, ther nys no more to saye. .
     The nexte houre of Mars folwynge this,
Arcite unto the temple walked is 1510
Of fierse Mars, to doon his sacrifise,
With alle the rites of his payen wise.
With pitous herte and heih devocioun,
Right thus to Mars he sayde his orisoun:
"O stronge god, that in the regnes colde 1515
Of Trace honoured art and lord y-holde,
And hast in every regne and every londe
Of armes al the bridel in thyn honde,
And hem fortunest as the lust devyse,
Accept of me my pitous sacrifise. 1520
If so be that my youthe may deserve,
And that my might be worthi for to serve
Thy godhede that I may ben on of thine,
Then praye I the to rewe upon my pyne.
For thilke peyne, and thilke hoote fyre, 1525
In which thou whilom brentest for desyre;

.   .   .   .
.   .   .   .
.   .   .   .
.   .   .   . 1530

1507. *The nexte waye*, the nearest way.
1510. *Walked is*, has walked.

. . . .
. . . .

For thilke sorwe that was in thin herte,
Have reuthe as wel upon my peynes smerte.
I am *y*ong and unkonnyng, as thou wost, 1535
And as I trowe, with love offended most,
That evere was eny lyves creature;
For sche, that doth me al this wo endure,
Ne reccheth nevere wher I synke or fleete.
And wel I woot, or sche me mercy heete, 1540
I moot with strengthe wynne hire in the place;
And wel I wot, withouten help or grace
Of the, ne may my strengthe nought avaylle.
Then help me, lord, to-morwe in my bataylle,
For thilke fyr that whilom brente the, 1545
As wel as thilke fir now brenneth me;
And do that I to-morwe have victorie.
Myn be the travaille, and thin be the glorie.
Thy soverein temple wol I most honouren
Of any place, and alway most labouren 1550
In thy plesaunce and in thy craftes stronge.
And in thy temple I wol my baner honge,
And alle the armes of my compainye;
And everemore, unto that day I dye,
Eterne fyr I wol biforn the fynde. 1555
And eek to this avow I wol me bynde:
My berd, myn heer that hangeth longe adoun,
That nevere *y*it ne felte offensioun
Of rasour ne of schere, I wol the *y*ive,
And be thy trewe servaunt whil I lyve. 1560
Now lord, have rowthe uppon my sorwes sore,
*Y*if me the victorie, I aske the no more."
    The preyere stynte of Arcita the stronge,
The rynges on the temple dore that honge,
And eek the dores, clatereden ful faste, 1565
Of which Arcita somwhat hym agaste.

1537. *Lyves creature*, creature alive, living creature.
1547. *Do*, bring it about, cause it to come to pass.

The fyres brende upon the auter brighte,
That it gan al the temple for to lighte;
And swote smel the ground anon upyaf,
And Arcita anon his hand up-haf,   1570
And more encens into the fyr he caste,
With othre rites mo; and atte laste
The statue of Mars bigan his hauberk rynge.
And with that soun he herde a murmurynge
Ful lowe and dym, that sayde thus, " Victorie."   1575
For which he yaf to Mars honour and glorie.
And thus with joye, and hope wel to fare,
Arcite anoon unto his inne is fare,
As fayn as fowel is of the brighte sonne.
And right anon such stryf ther is bygonne   1580
For thilke grauntyng, in the hevene above,
Bitwixe Venus the goddesse of love,
And Mars the sterne god armypotente,
That Jupiter was busy it to stente;
Til that the pale Saturnus the colde,   1585
That knew so manye of aventures olde,
Fond in his olde experience an art,
That he ful sone hath plesed every part.
As soth is sayd, eelde hath gret avantage,
In eelde is bothe wisdom and usage;   1590
Men may the olde at-renne, but nat at-rede.
Saturne anon, to stynte stryf and drede,
Al be it that it is agayn his kynde,
Of al this stryf he gan remedye fynde.
" My deere doughter Venus," quod Saturne,   1595
" My cours, that hath so wyde for to turne,

1579. As joyful as the bird is of the bright sun. So in Piers Pl., B. x. 153
1591. Men may outrun old age, but not outwit (surpass its counsel).
1593. *Agayn his kynde.*—According to the Compost of Ptolemeus, Saturn
     was influential in producing strife: " And the children of the sayd
     Saturne shall be great jangeleres and chyders, . . . and they wil
     never forgyve tyll they be revenged of theyr quarell."
1596. *My cours.*—The course of the planet *Saturn.* This refers to the orbit
     of Saturn, supposed to be the largest of all. So it was till Uranus
     and Neptune were discovered. (Skeat.)

Hath more power than woot eny man.
Myn is the drenchyng in the see so wan;
Myn is the prisoun in the derke cote;
Myn is the stranglyng and hangyng by the throte; 1600
The murmure, and the cherles rebellynge,
The groyning, and the pryvé empoysonynge :
I do vengeance and pleyn correctioun,
Whiles I dwelle in the signe of the lyoun.
Myn is the ruyne of the hihe halles,   1605
The fallyng of the toures and of the walles
Upon the mynour or the carpenter.
I slowh Sampsoun in schakyng the piler
And myne ben the maladies colde,
The derke tresoun, and the castes olde;   1610
Myn lokyng is the fader of pestilence.
Now wep nomore, I schal don diligence
That Palamon, that is thyn owne knight,
Schal have his lady, as thou hast him hight.
Though Mars schal helpe his knight, yet natheles 1615
Bitwixe you ther moot som tyme be pees,
Al be ye nought of oo complexioun,
That causeth al day such divisioun.
I am thin ayel, redy at thy wille;
Wep thou nomore, I wol thi lust fulfille."   1620
Now wol I stynten of the goddes above,
Of Mars, and of Venus goddesse of love,
And telle you, as pleinly as I can,
The gret effect for which that I bigan.
  Gret was the feste in Athenes that day,   1625
And eek the lusty sesoun of that May
Made every wight to ben in such plesaunce,
That al that Monday jousten they and daunce,
And spenden hit in Venus heigh servise.
But by the cause that they schulde arise   1630

1597. *More power*.—The Compost of Ptolemeus says of Saturn, " He is
myghty of hymself. . . . It is more than xxx yere or he may
ronne his course. . . . Whan he doth reygne, there is moche
debate."

Erly for to seen the grete fight,
Unto their reste wente they at nyght.
And on the morwe whan that day gan sprynge,
Of hors and herneys noyse and clateryge
Ther was in the hostelryes al aboute;   1635
And to the paleys rood ther many a route
Of lordes, upon steedes and palfreys.
Ther mayst thou seen devysyng of herneys
So uncowth and so riche, and wrought so wel
Of goldsmithrye, of browdyng, and of steel;   1640
The scheldes brighte, testers, and trappures;
Gold-beten helmes, hauberkes, cote-armures;
Lordes in paramentz on here courseres,
Knightes of retenue, and eek squyeres
Naylyng the speres, and helmes bokelynge,   1645
Giggyng of scheeldes, with layneres lasynge;
Ther as need is, they were nothing ydel;
The fomy steedes on the golden bridel
Gnawyng, and faste the armurers also
With fyle and hamer prikyng to and fro;   1650
Yemen on foote, and communes many oon
With schorte staves, thikke as they may goon;
Pypes, trompes, nakeres, clariounes,
That in the bataille blowe bloody sownes;
The paleys ful of peples up and doun,   1655
Heer thre, ther ten, holdyng here questioun,
Dyvynyng of thise Thebane knightes two.
Somme seyden thus, somme seyde it schal be so;
Somme heelde with him with the blake berd,   1659
Somme with the balled, somme with the thikke herd:
Somme sayde he lokede grym and he wolde fighte;
He hath a sparth of twenti pound of wighte.
Thus was the halle ful of divynynge,
Longe after that the sonne gan to springe.
The grete Theseus that of his sleep awaked   1665
With menstralcye and noyse that was maked,
Held yit the chambre of his paleys riche,
Til that the Thebane knyghtes bothe i-liche

Honoured weren into the paleys fet.
Duk Theseus was at a wyndow set, 1670
Arrayed right as he were a god in trone.
The peple preseth thider-ward ful sone
Him for to seen, and doon heigh reverence,
And eek to herkne his hest and his sentence.
An heraud on a skaffold made an hoo, 1675
Til al the noyse of the peple was i-do;
And whan he sawh the peple of noyse al stille,
Tho schewede he the mighty dukes wille.
    " The lord hath of his heih discrecioun
Considered, that it were destruccioun 1680
To gentil blood, to fighten in the gyse
Of mortal bataille now in this emprise;
Wherfore to schapen that they schuln not dye,
He wol his firste purpos modifye.
No man therfore, up peyne of los of lyf, 1685
No maner schot, ne pollax, ne schort knyf
Into the lystes sende, or thider brynge;
Ne schort swerd for to stoke, with point bytynge
No man ne drawe, ne bere by his side.
Ne no man schal unto his felawe ryde 1690
But oon cours, with a scharpe ygrounde spere;
Foyne if him lust on foote, himself to were.
And he that is at meschief, schal be take,
And nat slayn, but be brought unto the stake,
That schal ben ordeyned on eyther syde; 1695
But thider he schal by force, and ther abyde.
And if so falle, the cheventein be take
On eyther side, or elles sle his make,
No lenger schal the turneyinge laste.
God spede you; go forth and ley on faste. 1700
With long swerd and with mace fight your fille.
Goth now youre way; this is the lordes wille."
    The voice of peple touchede the hevene,
So lowde cride thei with mery stevene :

1688. Nor short sword having a *biting* (sharp) point to stab with.

"God save such a lord that is so good,   1705
He wilneth no destruccioun of blood!"
Up gon the trompes and the melodye.
And to the lystes ryt the compainye
By ordynaunce, thurghout the cité large,
Hanged with cloth of gold, and not with sarge.   1710
Ful lik a lord this noble duk gan ryde,
These tuo Thebanes upon eyther side;
And after rood the queen, and Emelye,
And after that another compainye,
Of oon and other after here degré.   1715
And thus they passen thurghout the cité,
And to the lystes come thei by tyme.
It nas not of the day yet fully pryme,
Whan set was Theseus ful riche and hye,
Ypolita the queen and Emelye,   1720
And other ladyes in degrees aboute.
Unto the seetes preseth al the route;
And west-ward, thurgh the yates under Marte,
Arcite, and eek the hundred of his parte,
With baner red ys entred right anoon;   1725
And in that selve moment Palamon
Is under Venus, est-ward in the place,
With baner whyt, and hardy cheere and face.
    In al the world, to seeken up and doun,
So evene withouten variacioun,   1730
Ther nere suche compainyes tweye.
For ther nas noon so wys that cowthe seye,
That any hadde of other avauntage
Of worthinesse, ne of estaat, ne age,
So evene were they chosen for to gesse.   1735
And in two renges faire they hem dresse.
Whan that here names rad were everychon,
That in here nombre gile were ther noon,
Tho were the yates schet, and cride was loude:
"Doth now your devoir, yonge knightes proude!"   1740
The heraudes lafte here prikyng up and doun;
Now ryngen trompes loude and clarioun;

Ther is nomore to sayn, but west and est
In gon the speres ful sadly in arest;
In goth the scharpe spore into the side.　　　1745
Ther seen men who can juste, and who can ryde;
Ther schyveren schaftes upon scheeldes thykke;
He fecleth thurgh the herte-spon the prikke.
Up springen speres twenty foot on highte;
Out goon the swerdes as the silver brighte.　　1750
The helmes thei to-hewen and to-schrede;
Out brest the blood, with sterne stremes reede.
With mighty maces the bones thay to-breste.
He thurgh the thikkeste of the throng gan threste.
Ther stomblen steedes stronge, and doun goon alle.
He rolleth under foot as doth a balle.　　　1756
He foyneth on his feet with his tronchoun,
And he him hurtleth with his hors adoun.
He thurgh the body is hurt, and siththen take
Maugre his heed, and brou*ght* unto the stake,　1760
As forward was, right ther he moste abyde.
Another lad is on that other syde.
And som tyme doth hem Theseus to reste,
Hem to refreissche, and drinken if hem leste.
Ful ofte a-day han thise Thebanes two　　　1765
Togidere y-met, and wrought his felawe woo;
Unhorsed hath ech other of hem tweye.
Ther nas no tygre in the vale of Galgopheye,
Whan that hire whelpe is stole, whan it is lite,

1744. In go the spears full firmly into the *rest;*—i.e. the spears were
　　couched ready for the attack. See Glossary, s. v. *Arrest.*
1756–7. *be . . . he* = one . . . another.
1757. *Feet.* Some MSS. read *foot,* but Tyrwhitt proposed to read *foo,*
　　foe, enemy. See l. 1692.
1766. *Wrought . . . woo,* done harm.
1768. *Galgopheye.* This word is variously written *Colaphey, Galgaphey,
　　Galapey.* There was a town called *Galapha* in Mauritania Tin-
　　gitana, upon the river Malva (Cellar. Geog. Ant. vii. p. 935),
　　which perhaps may have given name to the vale here meant.
　　(Tyrwhitt.) But perhaps Chaucer was thinking of the Vale of
　　Gargaphie.

So cruel on the hunte, as is Arcite　　　　　1770
For jelous herte upon this Palamoun:
Ne in Belmarye ther nis so fel lyoun,
That hunted is, or for his hunger wood,
Ne of his preye desireth so the blood,
As Palamon to slen his foo Arcite.　　　　　1775
The jelous strokes on here helmes byte;
Out renneth blood on bothe here sides reede.
Some tyme an ende ther is of every dede;
For er the sonne unto the reste wente,
The stronge kyng Emetreus gan hente　　　1780
This Palamon, as he faught with Arcite,
And made his swerd depe in his flessch to byte;
And by the force of twenti is he take
Unyolden, and i-drawe unto the stake.
And in the rescous of this Palamoun　　　　1785
The stronge kyng Ligurge is born adoun;
And kyng Emetreus for al his strengthe
Is born out of his sadel a swerdes lengthe,
So hitte him Palamon er he were take;
But al for nought, he was brought to the stake.　1790
His hardy herte mighte him helpe nought;
He moste abyde whan that he was caught,
By force, and eek by composicioun.
Who sorweth now but woful Palamoun,
That moot no more gon agayn to fighte?　　1795
And whan that Theseus hadde seen this sighte,
Unto the folk that foughten thus echon
He cryde, "Hoo! no more, for it is doon!
I wol be trewe juge, and nought partye.
Arcyte of Thebes schal have Emelye,　　　1800
That by his fortune hath hire faire i-wonne."
Anoon ther is a noyse of peple bygonne
For joye of this, so lowde and heye withalle,
It semede that the listes scholde falle.
　　What can now fayre Venus doon above?　　1805
What seith sche now? what doth this queen of love?
But wepeth so, for wantyng of hire wille,

Til that hire teeres in the lystes fille;
Sche seyde: "I am aschamed douteles."
Saturnus seyde: "Dou*gh*ter, hold thy pees.   1810
Mars hath his wille, his knight hath al his boone,
And by myn heed thou schalt ben esed soone."
    The trompes with the lowde mynstralcye,
The herawdes, that ful lowde *y*olle and crye,
Been in here wele for joye of daun Arcyte.   1815
But herkneth me, and stynteth now a lite,
Which a miracle ther bifel anoon.
This fierse Arcyte hath of his helm ydoon,
And on a courser for to schewe his face,
He priketh endelonge the large place,   1820
Lokyng upward upon his Emelye;
And sche agayn him caste a frendlych ey*gh*e,
(For wommen, as to speken in comune,
Thay folwen al the favour of fortune)
And was al his cheere, as in his herte.   1825
Out of the ground a fyr infernal sterte,
From Pluto sent, at requeste of Saturne,
For which his hors for feere gan to turne,
And leep asyde, and foundrede as he leep;
And or that Arcyte may taken keep,   1830
He pighte him on the pomel of his heed,
That in the place he lay as he were deed,
His brest to-brosten with his sadel-bowe.
As blak he lay as eny col or crowe,
So was the blood y-ronnen in his face.   1835
Anon he was y-born out of the place
With herte soor, to Theseus paleys.
Tho was he corven out of his harneys,
And in a bed y-brought ful faire and blyve,

1817. *Which a*, what a, how great a.
1825. *Al his cheere* may mean "altogether his, in countenance," as she
     was really so in his heart; *or* "all his countenance was as joyful
     as it was in his heart."
1826. *Fyr.* Elles. reads *furye*.
1838. Then was he cut out of his armor.

For he was ɣit in memorye and on lyve,   1840
And alway crying after Emelye.
   Duk Theseus, with al his compainye,
Is comen hom to Athenes his cité,
With alle blysse and gret solempnité.
Al be it that this aventure was falle,   1845
He nolde nought disconforten hem alle.
Men seyde eek, that Arcita schal nought dye,
He schal ben heled of his maladye.
And of another thing they were as fayn,
That of hem alle was ther noon y-slayn,   ·   1850
Al were they sore hurt, and namely oon,
That with a spere was thirled his brest boon.
To othre woundes, and to broken armes,
Some hadde salves, and some hadde charmes,
Fermacyes of herbes, and eek save   1855
They dronken, for they wolde here lymes have.
For which this noble duk, as he wel can,
Conforteth and honoureth every man,
And made revel al the longe night,
Unto the straunge lordes, as was right.   1860
Ne ther was holden no disconfytynge,
But as a justes or a tourneyinge;
For sothly ther was no disconfiture,
For fallynge nis not but an aventure;
Ne to be lad with fors unto the stake   1865
Unyolden, and with twenty knightes take,
O persone allone, withouten moo,   ˋ
And haried forth by arme, foot, and too,

1840. *In memorye*, conscious.
1853. As a remedy *for* (to) other wounds, &c.
1854, 1855. *Charmes . . . save.* It may be observed that the salves,
    charms, and pharmacies of herbs were the principal remedies of
    the physician in the age of Chaucer. *Save* (*salvia*, the herb sage)
    was considered one of the most universally efficient mediæval
    remedies (Wright); whence the proverb of the school of Salerno,
    " Cur moriatur homo, dum salvia crescit in horto?"
1864. *Nis not but* = is only.
1867. *O persone*, one person.

And eek his steede dryven forth with staves,
With footmen, bothe yemen and eek knaves,   1870
It nas aretted him no vyleinye,
Ther may no man clepe it no cowardye.
  For which anon Duk Theseus leet crie,
To stynten alle rancour and envye,
The gree as wel of o syde as of other,   1875
And either side ylik as otheres brother;
And yaf hem yiftes after here degré,
And fully heeld a feste dayes thre;
And conveyede the kynges worthily
Out of his toun a journee largely.   1880
And hom wente every man the righte way,
Ther was no more, but "Farwel, have good day!"
Of this bataylle I wol no more endite,
But speke of Palamon and of Arcyte.
  Swelleth the brest of Arcyte, and the sore   1885
Encresceth at his herte more and more.   •
The clothred blood, for eny leche-craft,
Corrumpeth, and is in his bouk i-laft,
That nother veyne blood, ne ventusynge,
Ne drynke of herbes may ben his helpynge.   1890
The vertu expulsif, or animal,
Fro thilke vertu cleped natural,
Ne may the venym voyde, ne expelle.
The pypes of his longes gonne to swelle,
And every lacerte in his brest adoun   1895
Is schent with venym and corrupcioun.
Him gayneth nother, for to gete his lyf,
Vomyt upward, ne dounward laxatif;
Al is to-brosten thilke regioun,
Nature hath now no dominacioun.   1900
And certeynly ther nature wil not wirche,
Farwel phisik; go ber the man to chirche.
This al and som, that Arcyta moot dye,

1878. *Dayes thre.* Wright says the period of three days was the usual
    duration of a feast among our early forefathers.
1903. *This al and som,* one and all *said* this—that Arcite must die.

For which he sendeth after Emelye,
And Palamon, that was his cosyn deere.   1905
Than seyde ne thus, as ye schul after heere.
     " Naught may the woful spirit in myn herte
Declare o poynt of alle my sorwes smerte
To you, my lady, that I love most;
But I byquethe the service of my gost   1910
To you aboven every creature,
Syn that my lyf ne may no lenger dure.
Allas, the woo ! allas, the peynes stronge,
That I for you have suffred, and so longe !
Allas, the deth ! allas, myn Emelye !   1915
Allas, departyng of our compainye !
Allas, myn hertes queen ! allas, my wyf !
Myn hertes lady, endere of my lyf !
What is this world? what asken men to have ?
Now with his love, now in his colde grave   1920
Allone withouten eny compainye.
Farwel, my swete foo ! myn Emelye !
And softe tak me in youre armes tweye,
For love of God, and herkneth what I seye.
     I have heer with my cosyn Palamon   1925
Had stryf and rancour many a day a-gon,
For love of yow, and for my jelousie.
And Jupiter so wis my sowle gye,
To speken of a servaunt proprely,
With alle circumstaunces trewely,   1930
That is to seyn, trouthe, honour, and knighthede,
Wysdom, humblesse, estaat, and hey kynrede,
Fredam, and al that longeth to that art,
So Jupiter have of my soule part,
As in this world right now ne knowe I non .   1935
So wortdy to be loved as Palamon,
That serveth you, and wol don al his lyf.
And if that evere ye schul ben a wyf,
Foryet not Palamon, the gentil man."

Some editors explain the phrase as *this* (is) *the al and som*, i.e.
this is the short and long of it.

And with that word his speche faille gan,   1940
For fro his feete up to his brest was come
The cold of deth, that hadde him overcome.
And yet, moreover, for in his armes two
The vital strengthe is lost, and al ago.
Only the intellect, withouten more,   1945
That dwellede in his herte sik and sore,
Gan fayllen, when the herte felte deth,
Dusken his eyghen two, and faylleth breth.
But on his lady yit caste he his eye;
His laste word was, " Mercy, Emelye !"   1950
His spiryt chaungede hous, and wente ther,
As I came nevere, I can nat tellen wher.
Therfore I stynte, I nam no dyvynistre;
Of soules fynde I not in this registre,
Ne me ne list thilke opynyons to telle   1955
Of hem, though that thei writen wher they dwelle.
Arcyte is cold, ther Mars his soule gye;
Now wol I speke forth of Emelye.
    Shrighte Emelye, and howleth Palamon,
And Theseus his suster took anon   1960
Swownyng, and bar hire fro the corps away.
What helpeth it to taryen forth the day,
To tellen how sche weep bothe eve and morwe ?
For in swich caas wommen can han such sorwe,
Whan that here housbonds ben from hem ago,   1965
That for the more part they sorwen so,
Or elles fallen in such maladye,
That atte laste certeynly they dye.
    Infynyte been the sorwes and the teeres
Of olde folk, and folk of tendre yeeres,   1970
In al the toun, for deth of this Theban,
For him ther weepeth bothe child and man;
So gret a wepyng was ther noon certayn,

1942. *Overcome.* Tyrwhitt reads *overnome*, overtaken, the p.p. of *over nimen.*

1957. *Ther Mars, &c.,* O that Mars would, &c.; may Mars, &c.

1964. *Such sorwe,* so great sorrow.

Whan Ector was i-brought, al fressh i-slayn,
To Troye; allas! the pité that was ther,   1975
Cracchyng of cheekes, rending eek of heer.
"Why woldestow be deed," thise wommen crye,
"And haddest gold ynowgh, and Emelye?"
No man ne mighte gladen Theseus,
Savyng his olde fader Egeus,   1980
That knew this worldes transmutacioun,
As he hadde seen it ternen up and doun,
Joye after woo, and woo after gladnesse:
And schewede hem ensamples and liknesse.
  "Right as ther deyde nevere man," quod he,   1985
"That he ne lyvede in erthe in som degree,
Right so ther lyvede nevere man," he seyde,
"In all this world, that some tyme he ne deyde.
This world nys but a thurghfare ful of woo,
And we ben pilgryms, passyng to and fro;   1990
Deth is an ende of every worldly sore."
And over al this yit seide he mochel more
To this effect, ful wysly to enhorte
The peple, that they schulde him reconforte.
  Duk Theseus, with al his busy cure,   1995
Cast now wher that the sepulture,
Of good Arcyte may best y-maked be,
And eek most honurable in his degré.
And atte laste he took conclusioun,
That ther as first Arcite and Palamon   2000
Hadden for love the bataille hem bytwene,
That in that selve grove, swoote and greene,
Ther as he hadde his amorouse desires,
His compleynte, and for love his hoote fyres,
He wolde make a fyr, in which thoffice   2005
Of funeral he mighte al accomplice;
And leet comaunde anon to hakke and hewe
The okes olde, and leye hem on a rewe
In culpons wel arrayed for to brenne,
His officers with swifte feet they renne,   2010
And ryde anon at his comaundement.

And after this, Theseus hath i-sent
After a beer, and it al overspradde
With cloth of gold, the richeste that he hadde.
And of the same suyte he cladde Arcyte;   2015
Upon his hondes hadde he gloves white;
Eek on his heed a coroune of laurer grene,
And in his hond a swerd ful bright and kene.
He leyde him bare the visage on the beere,
Therwith he weep that pité was to heere.   2020
And for the peple schulde seen him alle,
Whan it was day he broughte him to the halle,
That roreth of the crying and of the soun.
  Tho cam this woful Theban Palamoun,
With flotery berd, and ruggy asshy heeres,   2025
In clothes blake, y-dropped al with teeres;
And, passyng othere of wepyng, Emelye,
The rewfulleste of al the compainye.
In as moche as the service schulde be
The more noble and riche in his degré,   2030
Duk Theseus leet forth thre steedes brynge,
That trapped were in steel al gliterynge,
And covered with the armes of daun Arcyte.
Upon thise steedes, that weren grete and white,
Ther seeten folk, of which oon bar his scheeld,   2035
Another his spere up in his hondes heeld;
The thridde bar with him his bowe Turkeys,
Of brend gold was the caas and eek the herneys;
And riden forth a paas with sorweful cheere
Toward the grove, as ye schul after heere.   2040
The nobleste of the Grekes that ther were
Upon here schuldres carieden the beere,
With slake paas, and eyghen reede and wete,
Thurghout the cité, by the maister streete,
That sprad was al with blak, and wonder hye   2045
Right of the same is al the strete i-wrye.
Upon the right hond wente old Egeus,

2027. And surpassing others in weeping came Emily.

And on that other syde duk Theseus,
With vessels in here hand of gold wel fyn,
Al ful of hony, mylk, and blood, and wyn;   2050
Eek Palamon, with ful gret compainye;
And after that com woful Emelye,
With fyr in hond, as was that time the gyse,
To do thoffice of funeral servise.

Heygh labour, and ful gret apparaillynge   2055
Was at the service and the fyr makynge,
That with his grene top the hevene raughte,
And twenty fadme of brede tharmes straughte;
This is to seyn, the boowes were so brode.
Of stree first ther was leyd ful many a loode.   2060
But how the fyr was maked up on highte,
And eek the names how the trees highte,
As ook, fyrre, birch, asp, alder, holm, popler,
Wilwe, elm, plane, assch, box, chesteyn, lynde, laurer,
Maple, thorn, beech, hasel, ew, whyppyltre,   2065
How they weren feld, schal nought be told for me;
Ne how the goddes ronnen up and doun,
Disheryt of here habitacioun,
In which they woneden in reste and pees,   ·
Nymphes, Faunes, and Amadrydes;   2070
Ne how the beestes and the briddes alle
Fledden for feere, whan the woode was falle;
Ne how the ground agast was of the lighte,
That was nought wont to seen the sonne brighte;
Ne how the fyr was couched first with stree,   2075
And thanne with drye stykkes cloven a three,
And thanne with grene woode and spicerie,
And thanne with cloth of gold and with perrye,
And gerlandes hangyng with ful many a flour,
The myrre, thencens with al so greet odour;   2080
Ne how Arcyte lay among al this,
Ne what richesse aboute his body is;
Ne how that Emelye, as was the gyse,

2070. *Amadrydes* is a corruption of *Hamadryades*.

Putte in the fyr of funeral servise;
Ne how she swownede when men made the fyr,   2085
Ne what sche spak, ne what was hire desir;
Ne what jewels men in the fyr tho caste,
Whan that the fyr was gret and brente faste;
Ne how summe caste here scheeld, and summe here
    spere,
And of here vestimentz, whiche that they were,   2090
And cuppes ful of wyn, and mylk, and blood,
Into the fyr, that brente as it were wood;
Ne how the Grekes with an huge route
Thre tymes ryden al the fyr aboute
Upon the lefte hond, with an heih schoutyng,   2095
And thries with here speres clateryng;
And thries how the laydes gonne crye;
Ne how that lad was hom-ward Emelye;
Ne how Arcyte is brent to aschen colde;
Ne how that liche-wake was y-holde   2100
Al thilke night, ne how the Grekes pleye
The wake-pleyes, ne kepe I nat to seye;
Who wrastleth best naked, with oylle enoynt,
Ne who that bar him best in no disjoynt.
I wol not tellen eek how that they goon   2105
Hom til Athenes whan the pley is doon.
But schortly to the poynt than wol I wende,
And maken of my longe tale an ende.

   By processe and by lengthe of certyn yeres
Al stynted is the moornyng and the teeres   2110
Of Grekes, by oon general assent.
Than semede me ther was a parlement
At Athens, upon certeyn poyntz and cas;
Among the whiche poyntes yspoken was
To han with certyn contrees alliaunce,   2115
And han fully of Thebans obeissaunce.
For which this noble Theseus anon
Let senden after gentil Palamon,

2085. *Men made the fyr* (Harl.); *maad was the fire* (Corp. Pet.).
2104. *In no disjoynt*, with no disadvantage.

Unwist of him what was the cause and why;
But in his blake clothes sorwefully   2120
He cam at his comaundement in hye.
Tho sente Theseus for Emelye.
Whan they were set, and hust was al the place,
And Theseus abyden hadde a spacè
Or eny word cam fro his wyse brest,   2125
His eyen sette he ther as was his lest,
And with a sad visage he sykede stille,
And after that right thus he seide his wille.
" The firste moevere of the cause above,
Whan he first made the fayre cheyne of love,   2130
Gret was theffect, and heigh was his ententc;
Wel wiste he why, and what therof he mente;
For with that faire cheyne of love he bond
The fyr, the eyr, the water, and the lond
In certeyn boundes, that they may not flee;   2135
That same pyrnce and moevere eek," quod he,
" Hath stabled, in this wrecched world adoun,
Certeyne dayes and duracioun
To alle that ben engendred in this place,
Over the whiche day they may nat pace,   2140
Al mowe they yit tho dayes wel abregge;
Ther needeth non auctorité tallegge;
For it is preved by experience,
But that me lust declare my sentence.
Than may men by this ordre wel discerne,   2145
That thilke moevere stable is and eterne.'
Wel may men knowe, but it be a fool,
That every part deryveth from his hool.
For nature hath nat take his bygynnyng
Of no partye ne cantel of a thing,   2150
But of a thing that parfyt is and stable,
Descendyng so, til it be corumpable.
And therfore of his wyse purveiaunce
He hath so wel biset his ordinaunce,

2133-2135. *That faire cheyne of love.* This sentiment is taken from
Boethius, lib. ii. met. 8.

That spices of thinges and progressiouns   2155
Schullen endure by successiouns,
And nat eterne be withoute lye:
This maistow understande and sen at eye.
 "Lo the ook, that hath so long a norisschynge
Fro tyme that it gynneth first to springe,   2160
And hath so long a lyf, as we may see,
Yet atte laste wasted is the tree.
 "Considereth eek, how that the harde stoon
Under oure feet, on which we trede and goon,
Yit wasteth it, as it lith by the weye.   2165
The brode ryver somtyme wexeth dreye.
The grete townes seen we wane and wende.
Then may ye see that al this thing hath ende.
 "Of man and womman sen we wel also,
That nedeth in oon of thise termes two,   2170
This is to seyn, in youthe or elles age,
He moot ben deed, the kyng as schal a page;
Som in his bed, som in the deepe see,
Some in the large feeld, as men may se.
Ther helpeth naught, al goth that ilke weye.   2175
Thanne may I seyn that al this thing moot deye.
What maketh this but Jupiter the kyng?
The which is prynce and cause of alle thing,
Convertyng al unto his propre welle,
From which it is deryved, soth to telle.   2180
And here agayns no creature on lyve
Of no degré avaylleth for to stryve.
 "Than is it wisdom, as it thinketh me,
To maken vertu of necessité,
And take it wel, that we may nat eschue,   2185
And namelyche that to us alle is due.

2158. *Sen at eye*, see at a glance.
2184. So in Troilus, iv. 1558: "Thus maketh vertu of necessite;" and
     in Squire's Tale, pt. ii. l. 247: "That I made vertu of necessite."
     Cp. Horace, Carm. i. 24:
              "Durum! sed lenius fit patientia
               Quidquid corrigere est nefas."

And who so gruccheth aught, he doth folye,
And rebel is to him that al may gye.
And certeynly a man hath most honour
To deyen in his excellence and flour,   2190
Whan he is siker of his goode name.
Than hath he doon his freend, ne him, no schame,
And gladder oughte his freend ben of his deth,
Whan with honour up-*y*olden is his breth,
Thanne whan his name appalled is for age;   2195
For al forgeten is his vasselage.
Thanne is it best, as for a worthi fame,.
To dyen whan a man is best of name.
The contrarye of al this is wilfulnesse.
Why grucchen we? why have we hevynesse,   2200
That good Arcyte, of chyvalrye the flour,
Departed is, with dueté and honour
Out of this foule prisoun of this lyf?
Why grucchen heer his cosyn and his wyf
Of his welfare that lovede hem so wel?   2205
Can he hem thank? nay, God woot, never a del,
That bothe his soule and eek hemself offende,
And *y*et they mowe here lustes nat amende.
    "What may I conclude of this longe serye,
But after wo I rede us to be merye,   2210
And thanke Jupiter of al his grace?
And or that we departe fro this place,
I rede that we make, of sorwes two,
O parfyt joye lastyng evere mo: `
And loketh now wher most sorwe is her-inne,   2215
Ther wol we first amenden and bygynne.
    "Suster," quod he, "this is my fulle assent,
With al thavys heer of my parlement,
That gentil Palamon, *y*oure owne knight,
That serveth *y*ow with herte, wille, and might,   2220
And evere hath doon, syn that ye fyrst him knewe,

2210. Cp. "The time renneth toward right fast,
      Joy cometh after when the sorrow is past."
          (Hawes' Pastime of Pleasure. ed. Wright, p. 148.)

That *y*e schul of *y*oure grace upon him rewe,
And take him for *y*oure housbond and for lord:
Leen me *y*oure hand, for this is oure acord.
Let.see now of *y*oure wommanly pité.   2225
He is a kynges brother sone, pardee;
And though he were a poure bacheler,
Syn he hath served *y*ou so many a yeer,
And had for *y*ou so gret adversité,
It moste be considered, leeveth me.   2230
For gentil mercy aughte to passe right."
Than seyde he thus to Palamon the knight;
"I trowe ther needeth litel sermonyng
To maken *y*ou assente to this thing.
Com neer, and tak *y*oure lady by the hond."   2235
Bitwixen hem was i-maad anon the bond,
That highte matrimoyne or mariage,
By al the counseil and the baronage.
And thus with alle blysse and melodye
Hath Palamon i-wedded Emelye.   2240
And God, that al this wyde world hath wrought,
Sende him his love, that hath it deere a-bought.
For now is Palamon in alle wele,
Lyvynge in blisse, in richesse, and in hele,
And Emelye him loveth so tendrely,   2245
And he hire serveth al so gentilly,
That nevere was ther no word hem bitweene
Of jelousye, or any other teene.
Thus endeth Palamon and Emelye;
And God save al this fayre compainye !   2250

2231. *Aughte to passe right*, should surpass mere equity or justice.

GLOSSARY.

Numbers refer to lines. The following are the chief contractions used:

A.S.	= Anglo-Saxon.	Lat.	= Latin.
Dan.	= Danish.	O.E.	= Old English.
Du.	= Dutch.	O.Fr.	= Old French.
Fr.	= French.	O.H.Ger.	= Old High German.
Ger.	= German.	Prov. Engl.	= Provincial English.
Gr.	= Greek.	Sp.	= Spanish.
It.	= Italian.	Sw.	= Swedish.

A, one, single. A.S. *an*, Ger. *ein*, one; Eng. indef. article *an* or *a*.

A, in, on; cp. *a-night*, 184, *a day*, daily, 1765; *a-three*, in three, 2076. Cp. Mod. Eng. *a-foot*, *afraid*, *a-hunting*, *a-building*, &c. A.S. and O.S. *an*, in, on. It is still used in the South of England.

Abide, abiden, abyden, abide, delay, wait for, await, 69, 2124. A.S. *abidan*, to wait, remain.

Able, fit, capable, adapted: Lat. *habilis* (Lat. *habeo*, to have), convenient, fit: O.Fr. *habile*, able, expert, fit.

Abood, delay. 107. See *Abide*.

Aboughte, atoned for, suffered for, 1445, 2240. A.S. *abicgan*, to redeem, pay the purchase-money, to pay the penalty (from *bycgan*, to buy). Cp. the modern expression "to buy it dear." Shakespeare and Milton have, from similarity of sound, given the sense of *abye* to the verb *abide*, as in the following examples:

"If it be found so, some will dear *abide* it. (Julius Cæsar.)

"Disparage not the faith thou dost not know.

"Lest to thy peril thou *abidest*, dear." (Mids. Night's Dream.)

"How dearly I *abide* that boast in vain." (Paradise Lost.)

Aboven, above.

Abrayde, abreyde, started (suddenly), awoke. A.S. *brægdan*, to move, turn, weave. Shakespeare uses *braid* = of deceitful manner.

Abregge, to shorten, *abridge*. 2141. Fr. *a-breger;* Lat. *abbreviare*.

Accomplice, to accomplish, 2006.

Accordant, acordaunt, according to, agreeing, suitable.

Accorde, acorde, agreement, decision.

Accorde, acorde, to agree, suit, decide. Fr. *accorder*, to agree (from Lat. *cor*, the heart).

Achate, purchase. O.Fr. *achepter*, to buy; Fr. *acheter*.

Achatour, purchaser, caterer.

Acorded, agreed, 356.

Acqueyntaunce, aqueyntaunce, acquaintance.

Ademauntz, adamant, 1132. Gr. ἀ-δάμας (a privative, δαμάω, to tame, subdue), the hardest metal, probably steel (also the diamond); whence Eng. *adamantine.*

Adoun, adown, down, downwards below, 245.

Adrad, in great dread, afraid. Cp. O.E. *of-drad*, much afraid; where the prefix *of* is intensitive, like *for-*, Lat. *per-*.

Aferd, afered, afferd, in great fear, afraid, 660.

Affeccioun, affection, hope, 300.

Affermed, confirmed, 1491.

Affrayed, terrified, scared. Fr. *effrayer*, scare, appal; *effroi*, terror: whence *fray* and *affray.*

Affyle, to file, to polish. Fr. *affiler;* Lat. *filum*, a thread.

Afright, in fright, afraid. Ger. *Furcht*, fear.

Again, agayn, ageyn, again, against, towards, 929.

Agast, terrified, *aghast*, 1483.

Agaste, to be terrified, 1566.

Ago, agon, agoo, agoon, gone, past, 418, 924; the past participle of O.E. verb *agon*, to go, pass away. We also meet with *ygo* in the same sense, and some etymologists have erroneously supposed that the prefix *a-* is a corruption of *y-*.

Agrief, in grief. "To take *agrief*"

= to take it amiss, feel aggrieved, be displeased.

Al, all, whole (cp. *al a* = a whole, 58), quite wholly (cp. *al redy, al armed.* &c.).

Alauntz (or alauns), a species of dog, 1290. They were used for hunting the boar.

Al be, although.

Alder, alther, aller, of all (gen. pl. of *al*).

Ale-stake, a stake set up before an ale-house by way of sign.

Algate, always.

Alighte (p.p. *alight*), alighted, 125. Cp. the phrase " to *light* upon."

Alle, pl. of *al* (all).

Aller. See *Alder.*

Alliaunce, alliance, 2115. Fr. *allier*, to ally.

Als, also, as. These forms show that *as* is a contraction from *also.*

Alther. See *Alder.*

Amblere, a nag.

Amonges, amongst.

Amorwe, on the morrow.

Amounte, to amount, signify, denote, 1504.

Amyddes, amidst, in the middle, 1151.

And = *an*, if, 356.

Anhange, anhonge, to hang up.

Anlas (or anelace), a kind of knife or dagger, usually worn at the girdle.

Anon, anoon, *in one* (instant), anon.

Anoynt, enoynt, anointed.

Apayd, apayed, pleased, satisfied, 1010. Fr. *payer*, to satisfy. pay (Lat. *pacare*); whence O.E. *pay*, satisfaction, gratification, pleasure; Eng. *pay.*

Ape, metaphorically, a fool.

Apiked, trimmed. See *Pike.*

Apotecarie, apothecary.

Appalled, become weak, feeble, dead, 2195.

Apparaillyng, preparation, 2055. Fr. *appareiller*, to fit, suit; *pareil*, like; Lat. *par*, equal, like. The original meaning of *appareiller* is to join like to like.

Appetyt, desire, appetite, 822.

Arest, a support for the spear when couched for the attack, 1744. It is sometimes written *rest*.

Areste, to stop (a horse).

Aretted, ascribed, imputed, deemed, 1871. The A.S. *aretan* signifies to correct, set right.

Arive, arrival, or perhaps disembarkation (of troops). From Lat. *ad ripare*, to come to shore.

Arm-gret, as thick as a man's arm, 1287.

Armypotent, mighty in arms, 1124.

Array, state, situation, dress, equipage, 76.

Arraye, to set in order, dress, adorn, equip, 1188. It. *arredare*, to prepare, get ready.

Arreest, seizure, custody, 452.

Arrerage, arrears.

Arresten, to stop, seize.

Arsmetrike, arithmetic, 1040.

Arwe, arrow.

As, as if.

Aschen, asschen, ashes, 444.

Aseged, besieged, 23. Fr. *siege;* Lat. *obsidium*, the sitting down before a town in a hostile way.

Aslake, to moderate, appease, 902. A.S. *slacian*, relax, *slack;* *sleac*, slack; also *slack-lime*, *slag* of a furnace.

As-nouthe, as now, at present, 1406. See *Nouthe*.

Asonder, asunder.

Assaut, assault, 131. Fr. *assaillir*, to assail; *saillir*, to leap,

sally; Lat. *salire*, to leap, spring.

Assayed, tried, 953. Fr. *essayer*, to try, *essay*.

Assise, assize. Fr. *assire*. to set; (Lat. *assidere*); *assis*, set, seated; *assise*, a settled tax; *cour d'assize*, a court held on a set day

Assoillyng, absolution, acquittal. O.Fr. *assoiller*, Lat. *absolvere*, to loose from.

Assuren, to make sure, confirm, 1066.

Astat, astaat, estate, rank. See *Estat*.

Asterte, to escape, 737: p. p. 734. See *Sterte*.

Astoned, astonished, 1504. Lat. *attonare*, to thunder at, stun.

Astored, stored.

Asure, azure.

Athamaunte, adamant, 447.

Atrede, to surpass in council, outwit, 1591. *at-* = A.S. *æt*, of, from, out.

At-renne, outrun, 1391. See *Renne*.

Atte, at the.

Attempre, adj. temperate, moderate.

Atteyne, to attain, 385. Lat. *tangere*, to touch, *attingere*, to reach to.

Auctorité, authority; a text of Scripture, or some respectable writer, 2142.

Auctours, authors, writers of credit.

Auter, altar, 1047.

Avaunce, to be of advantage, be profitable.

Avaunt, boast, *vaunt*.

Avauntage, advantage, 435.

Avauntour, boaster.

Aventure, chance, luck, misfortune. Lat. *advenire*, to happen; whence, Eng. *peradventure*.

Avis, avys, advice, consideration, opinion, 1010.

Avisioun, avysoun, vision.

Avow, vow, promise, 1379.

Avoy, fie!

Awayt, watch. This is connected with *wake.* Eng. *watch, waits,* to *await.*

Awe, fear, dread.

Axe, to ask, 489.

Axyng, asking, demand, 968.

Ay, ever, aye.

Ayein, ayeins, ayens, again, back, against, towards, 651.

Ayel, a grandfather, 1619. Fr. *aïeul.*

Baar, bar, bore, carried. See *Bere.*

Bacheler, bachiller, an unmarried man, *bachelor,* a knight.

Bacoun, bacon.

Bailliff, bailiff.

Bak, back.

Bake = *baken,* baked.

Balled, bald, 1660. The original meaning seems to have been (1) shining, (2) white (as in *bald-faced* stag).

Bane, destruction, death, 239, 823.

Baner, a banner, 120, 1552.

Bar, bore, conducted.

Barbour, a barber. Lat. *barba,* the beard.

Bare, open, plain, 2019.

Bareyn, bareyne, barren, devoid of, 386, 1119.

Baronage, an assembly of barons, 2238. The root perhaps is identical with the Lat. *vir.* (Wedgwood.)

Barre, bar or bolt of a door, 217. Eng. *spar,* sibilated form of the root *bar* or *par,* which may be referred to O.N. *barr,* a tree.

Barres, ornaments of a girdle.

Batail, bataile, bataille, batayl, bataylle, battle, 130. Fr.

bataille, a battle. With the root *bat* are connected *battery, batter.*

Bataylld, embattled. Fr. *batillé, bastillé,* built as a bastile or fortress, furnished with turrets.

Bawdrick, *baudrick,* or *baldrick,* belt, or girdle, worn transversely.

Be, (1) to be, 1377; (2) been.

Bede, a bead (pl. *bedes*). A.S. *bead, gebed,* a prayer. "*Beads* were strung on a string, and originally used for the purpose of helping the memory in reciting a certain tale of prayers or doxologies. To bid one's *bedes* or *beads* was to say one's prayers."

Beem, bemys, beam, rafter (pl. *beemes*). A.S. *bedm,* a tree, stick, beam; Ger. *Baum.*

Beemes, trumpets, horns.

Been, (1) to be; (2) are; (3) been.

Beer, beere, a bier, 2013.

Beer, did bear.

Beest, best, a beast, 451.

Beete, to kindle, light, 1395. The literal meaning is to mend, repair.

Begger, beggere, a beggar. It signifies literally a *bag-bearer.* It must be borne in mind that the *bag* was a universal characteristic of the beggar.

Beggestere, a beggar, properly a female beggar.

Ben, (1) to be; (2) are; (3) been.

Benigne, kind.

Bent, declivity of a hill, a plain, open field, 1123.

Berd, berde, beard, 1272.

Bere, to bear, to carry, to conduct one's self, behave. Imper. *ber,* 1902.

Bere, a bear, 782.

Bere, to pierce, strike, 1398.

Berkyng, barking. With the

root *brak* are connected Eng. *bark*, *brag*, and *bray*.

Bersten, to burst, 1122.

Berstles, bristles.

Berye, a berry.

Beseken, to beseech, 60.

Best, beste, a beast, 1118.

Besy, busy, industrious, anxious.

Bet, better. A.S. *bet;* O.H. Ger. *baz*. See *Beete*.

Bete, (1) to beat; (2) beaten, or-namented. See *Ybete*.

Beth, (3d pers. sing. of *Ben*), is; (imp. pl.), be.

Betwix, betwixe, betwixt. The second element *-tweox* is connected with *two*, and occurs in be-*tween*.

Bewreye, to betray, 1371. See *Bywreye*.

Beyying, buying, *yy = gg*. Cp. O.E. *begge*, to buy.

Bibled, covered over with blood, 1114.

Bifalle, p.p. befallen; to befall, 947.

Bihight, promised.

Biholde, to behold, 1435.

Biknew, acknowledged, confessed.

Biloved, beloved.

Bisette, to employ, use, 2154.

Biside, bisides, beside, near, besides.

Bitweene, bytweene, between, 2246. See *Betwix*.

Bitwix, bitwixe, bytwixen, betwixt, between, 22.

Blak, black, 41, 1659. With this root are connected *bleak*, *bleach*.

Blede, to bleed, 943.

Bleynte, blenched, started back, 220.

Blis, blisse, bliss, 372.

Blisful, blessed, blissful.

Blive, blyve, quickly, forth-with, 1889.

Bocher, a butcher, 1167. Fr. *boucher*, from *boc*, a goat.

Bok (pl. *bokes*), a book.

Bokeler, buckler. Fr. *bouclier*, a shield with a central boss, from *boucle*, protuberance.

Bokelyng, buckling, 1645.

Boket, a bucket, 675.

Bole, bull; pl. *boles*, 1281.

Bond, bound, = O.E. *band* (pret. of *binden*), 2133.

Boon, boone, prayer, petition, *boon*.

Boon, bone (pl. *boones*), 319.

Boor, boar, 800.

Boot, boote, remedy. See *Beete*.

Boowes, boughs, 2059.

Boras, borax.

Bord, table.

Bord, joust, tournament.

Bore, p.p. born, 684.

Born, p.p. conducted.

Borwe, pledge, security, 764. Cp. Ger. *Bürge*, from *beorgan*, to protect (whence *borough*), a surety ; *bürgen*, to become a surety, to give bail for another. In the phrase "a snug *berth*," a berth on board ship. we have a derivative of the same root.

Botes, bootes, boots. " The boot appears to have originally been like the Irish brogue and Indian mocassin, a sort of bag of skin or leather, enveloping the foot and laced on the instep." (Wedgwood.)

Bothe, both, 983.

Botiler, butler. It is generally connected with *bouteille*, a bottle; but it is more probably connected with *buttery* and *butt*.

Botme, bottom.

Bouk, body, 1888. Icel. *bulka*, to swell; whence Eng. *bulk*, Prov. Eng. *bulch*. Cotgrave has

"*Bossé*, knobby, *bulked* or bumped out." With this root are connected Eng. *billow, bulge, bilge.*

Bour. A.S. *bur*, bower, inner chamber; Prov. Eng. *boor*, a parlor.

Bracer, armor for the arms.

Brak, broke, 610.

Bras, brass.

Brast, burst. It is sometimes written *barst.*

Braun, brawn, muscle (pl. *brawnes*), 1277.

Braunche, a branch, 209.

Brayde, started. See *Abrayde.*

Bred, breed, bread.

Breed, breede, breadth, 1112.

Breeme, fiercely, furiously, 841.

Breeth, breth, breath. In O.E. *bræth* signifies vapor, smell, also fervor, rage.

Breke, to break.

Brem, a fresh-water fish, bream.

Bremstoon, brimstone. O.E. *brenstone* = burning stone.

Bren, bran.

Brend, burnished, bright, 1304.

Brende, burnt, 1567. See *Brenne.*

Brenne, to burn, 1473. A.S. *brennan, bernan*. We have the same root in *brim*-stone.

Brenningly, fiercely, ardently, 706.

Brennyng, brennynge, burning, 138, 1142.

Brent, burnt, 1159.

Breres, briers, 674.

Brest, bursteth, 1752.

Brest, breste, breast.

Brest-plat, breast-plate, 1262.

Breste, to burst, 1752. See *Brast.*

Bretful, brimfull, 1306. See *Brede*, breadth.

Bretherhede, brotherhood, brothers of a religious order.

Briddes, birds. A.S. *brid*, a (young) bird; *brod*, a brood A.S. *bredan*, to nourish, keep warm. We have the same root in *brew* and *broth*. Shakespeare uses *bird* in its original sense in the following passage:

" Being fed by us, you used us so
　As that ungentle gull, the
　　cuckoo's *bird*,
Useth the sparrow."
　　　　　　　(1 Hen. IV. v. 1)

Broch, a brooch. Cp Lat. *brocchus*, a projecting tooth.

Brode, broad, 2166. See *Brood.*

Broke, broken. See *Breke.*

Brood, broode, brode, broad. See *Brede.*

Broode, broadly, plainly.

Brond, firebrand, 1481.

Brouke, to have the use of, enjoy, *brook.*

Broun, brown. Ger. *braun*, Fr. *brun*. It is perhaps connected with *brennan*, to burn.

Browded, braided, woven, 191. For the etymology see *Abrayde.*

Browdyng, embroidery, 1640.

Bulde, built, 690.

Bulte, to bolt (corn), sift meal.

Burdon, burden (of a song), a musical accompaniment. Sp. *bordon*, the bass of a stringed instrument, or of an organ.

Burgeys, citizen, burgess.

Burned, burnished, 1125. Fr. *brunir.*

Busynesse, bysynesse, labor, care, anxiety, 149.

But-if, unless.

By and by, separately, 153.

Bycause, because.

Byde, abide, remain, 718.

Byfel, byfil, befell, 152.

Byfore, byforen, byforn, before, 518.

Bygan, bigan, began, 690.

Bygonne, p.p. begun.

Bygynne, to begin.

Byholde, to behold, 443.

Byhote, promise, 996. See *Bihight*.

Byhynde, behind, 192.

Byjaped, deceived, befooled, 727. The root *jap* is connected with *gab*, *jab*, as in *gabble*, *jabber*.

Byknowe, to acknowledge, 698.

Byloved, beloved, 571.

Bynethe, beneath.

Bynne, bin, chest. It is sometimes written *bing*, and seems to have signified originally a heap.

Byquethe, to bequeath, 1910.

Byraft, bereft, 503.

Byside, beside, near.

Bysmotered, spotted, smutted.

Byt, (3d pers. sing. of *bidden*), bids.

Bythought, "am bethought," have thought of, have called to mind.

Bytwixe, betwixt, between.

Bywreye, make known, bewray, 1371.

Caas, case, condition, hap.

Caas, case, quiver, 1500.

Cacche, cachche, to catch, (pret. *caughte*). Fr. *chasser*, to drive out, *chase*.

Caitif, caytif, wretch, wretched, 66, 694. (Lat. *captivus*), a captive, a wretch.

Cam, came.

Can, (1) know, knows, 922.

Cantel, corner, cantle, 2150. O.Fr. *chantel*, *chanteau*, a corner, a lump. Cp. Icel. *kantr*, side; Dan. *kant*, edge.

Cappe, a cap, hood.

Care, sorrow, grief. *Careful*, sorrowful, 463. A.S. *caru*, Goth. *kara*.

Carf, carved (the pret. of *kerve*, to cut, *carve*). A.S. *ceorfan*, O. Fris. *kerva*, to cut.

Carl, a churl. A.S. *ceorl*, Icel. *karl*, a man. Cp. Sc. *carlin*, an old woman; Eng. *churl*, *churlish*.

Caroigne, carrion, 1155. Fr. *charogne*, It. *carogna*, from Lat. *caro*.

Carol, a round dance, 1073. *Carole*, to dance. Fr. *carole* (from Lat. *corolla*, the diminutive of *corona*). Robert of Brunne calls the circuit of Druidical stones a *karole*. By some it is derived from the Lat. *chorale*.

Carpe, to talk, discourse. Cp. Portug. *carpire*, to cry, weep.

Carte, chariot, cart, 1164. O.N. *karti*.

Cartere, charioteer, 1164.

Cas, case, condition, hap, chance, 216. See *Caas*.

Cast, casteth, 1996.

Cast, device, plot, 1610. It is connected with the vb. to *cast*. Cp. O.E. *turn*, a trick; Eng. "an *illturn*."

Caste, casten, to plan, devise, suppose, 1314.

Catapus, catapuce, a species of spurge.

Catel, wealth, goods, valuable property of any kind, *chattels*. O.Fr. *chatel*, *catel*, a piece of movable property, from Lat. *capitale*, whence *captale*, *catallum*, the principal sum in a loan (cp. Eng. *capital*). The Lat. *captale* was also applied to beasts of the farm, *cattle*.

Caughte, took. Cp. Eng. "caught cold." See *Cacche*.

Celle, a religious house, *cell*, 518.

Centaure, century, the name of an herb.

Cercles, circles, 1273.

Cerial, belonging to the species of oak called *Cerrus* (Lat.), 1432.

Certein, certeyn, certes, certain, certainly, indeed, 17.

Certeinly, certeynly, certainly.

Ceruce, white lead.

Chaffer, merchandise.

Champartye, a share of land; a partnership in power, 1091.

Champioun, a champion.

Chanterie, chaunterie, "An endowment for the payment of a priest to sing mass agreeably to the appointment of the founder."

Chapeleyne, a chaplain.

Chapman, a merchant. A.S. *ceapman*. See *Chaffer*.

Char, car, chariot, 1280. Fr. *char*, Lat. *carrus*; whence Fr. *charrier*, to carry; *charger*, to load, charge.

Charge, harm, 426, 1429, as in the phrase "it were no *charge*."

Chaunce, chance, hap, 894.

Chaunge, chaungen, to change.

Chaunterie. See *Chanterie*.

Cheef, chief, 199. Fr. *chef*, head; Lat. *caput*.

Cheer, cheere, chere, countenance, appearance, entertainment, cheer, 55.

Cherl, churl, 1601. See *Carl*.

Ches, imp. sing. *choose*, 737.

Chese, to choose.

Chesteyn, a chestnut-tree, 2064.

Cheventein, a chieftain, *captain*, 1697. See *Cheef*.

Chevisance, chevysaunce, gain, profit; also an agreement for borrowing money.

Cheyne, a chain, 2130.

Chiden, to chide.

Chikne, a chicken. The word *cock*, of which *chicken* is a diminutive, is evidently formed in imitation of the sound made by young birds. Cp. *chuck*, *chuckle*, &c.

Chirkyng, sb. shrieking, 1146. The O.E. *chirke* signifies "to make a noise like a bird," being a parallel form with *chirp*, and imitative of the sound made by birds.

Chivachie, a military expedition.

Chivalrie, chyvalrye, knighthood, the manners, exercises, and valiant exploits of a knight, 7, 20. Fr. *chevalerie*, from *chevalier*, a knight, a horseman; *cheval*, a horse.

Choys, choice. Fr. *choisir*, to choose. See *Chese*.

Chronique, a chronicle.

Cite, citee, a city.

Citole, a kind of musical instrument with chords, 1101.

Clapsed, clasped.

Clarioun, clarion, 1653.

Clarré, wine mixed with honey and spices, and afterwards strained till it was *clear*, 613. It was also called *Piment*.

Clatere, clatren, to clatter, 1501.

Cleer, cleere, adj. clear, adv. clearly, 204.

Clene, adj. clean, pure; adv. cleanly.

Clennesse, cleanness, purity (of life).

Clense, to cleanse.

Clepen, to call, cry, say.

Cleped, clept, called, 930.

Clerk, a man of learning, a student at the University.

Cloke, a cloak.

Clomben, climbed, ascended.

Cloos, close, shut.

Clos, enclosure, yard.

Clothred = *clottred*, clotted, 1887. We have the root-syllable in *clot* and *clod*. A.S. *clot*, clod. Eng.

cloud is evidently from the same source as *clod.*

Cloystre, a cloister.

Cofre, coffer, chest.

Col, coal, 1834. A.S. *col,* Icel. *kol,* Ger. *Kohle.*

Col-blak, coal-black, black as a coal, 1284.

Col-fox, a crafty fox.

Colere, choler.

Colers of, having collars of, 1294.

Comaunde, to command.

Comaundement, commandment, command, 2011.

Comen, p.p. come, 497.

Communes, commoners, common people, 1651.

Compaas, circle, 1031.

Còmpaignye, compainye, company.

Companable, companionable, sociable.

Compassyng, craft, contrivance, 1138.

Comper, gossip, a near friend.

Compleint, compleynt, complaint, 2004.

Complet, complete.

Compleyne, compleynen, to complain, 50.

Composicioun, agreement.

Comune, commune, common. *As in comune* = as in common; commonly, 393.

Condicionel, conditional.

Condicioun, condition.

Confort, comfort.

Conforte, to comfort, 858.

Confus, confused, confounded, 1372.

Conne, know, be able. See *Can, Con.*

Conscience, feeling, pity.

Conseil, conseyl, counsel, 283, 289.

Conserve, to preserve, 1471.

Contek, contest, 1145.

Contenaunce, countenance, 1058.

Contrarye, an opponent, adversary, foe, 1001.

Contre, contrie, country, 355.

Coote, cote, coat.

Coote-armour. See *Cote-armour.*

Cop, top of anything. Ger. *Kopf,* top, summit.

Cope, a cloak, cape.

Corage, heart, spirit, courage. Fr. *courage,* from Lat. *cor,* the heart.

Coroune, corowne, a crown, 964.

Corrumpe, to corrupt, 888.

Corumpable, corruptible, 2152.

Corven (p.p. of *kerve*), cut, 1838.

Cosin, cosyn, a cousin, kinsman, 273.

Cote, cottage. Cp. *sheep-cote, dove-cote.*

Cote, coat. O.Fr. *cote.*

Cote-armour, cote-armure, coote-armour, a coat worn over armor, upon which the armorial ensigns of the wearer were usually embroidered, 158, 1282.

Couched, cowched, (1) laid, (2) inlaid, trimmed, 1303, 2075.

Counseil, counsel, advice, 283.

Countrefete, counterfeit, imitate.

Cours, course, 836.

Courtepy, a sort of upper coat of a coarse material.

Couthe, cowde, cowthe, (1) could, (2) knew. See *Can.*

Covyne, *covin,* deceit. Literally a deceitful agreement between two parties to prejudice a third.

Cowardie, cowardice, 1872; from Lat. *cauda,* a tail. The real origin of the word is a metaphor from the proverbial timidity of a hare, which was called *couard* from its short tail. (Wedgwood.)

Cowde, could, knew how.

Coy, quiet.

Cracchyng, scratching, 1976.

Crafty, skilful, 1039.

Crien, cryen, to cry. *Crydestow* = criedst thou, 225.

Crisp, crispe, crisp, curled, 1307.

Croppe, crop, top, 674.

Croys, cross.

Crulle, curly, curled.

Cryke, creek.

Culpons, culpouns, shreds, bundles, logs.

Cuntre, country, 2009.

Cuppe, a cup.

Curat, a curate.

Cure, care, anxiety, 1995.

Curious, careful.

Curs, curse.

Curteis, curteys, courteous.

Curteisie, courtesy.

Cut, lot.

Daliaunce, gossip.

Damoysele, damsel.

Dampned, condemned, doomed, 317.

Dan, daun, Lord, was a title commonly given to monks, 521.

Dar, dare (1st pers. sing. present tense), 293. **Darst** (2d sing.), 282. **Dorste, durste** (pret.).

Darreyne, derreyne, to contest, fight out, decide by battle, *darraign,* 773.

Daunce, daunse, vb. to dance, sb. a dance, 1343, 1344.

Daunger, a dangerous situation, 991.

Daungerous, difficult, sparing.

Daunsynge, dancing, 1343.

Dawen, to dawn, 818.

Dawenynge, dawn, dawning.

Dayerie, dairy. See *Deye.*

Dayseye, a daisy. Chaucer defines *daisy* as the eye of the day, i.e., day's eye.

Debonaire, kind, gracious, 1424.

Dede (pret. of *don*), did, 891.

Dede, a deed.

Dede, deed, deede, dead, 84, 147.

Dedly, deedly, deadly, death-like, 55, 224.

Deduyt, pleasure, delight, 1319.

Deef, deaf.

Deel, a part. See *Del.*

Deepe, depe, deeply, 1782.

Deer, deere, dere, dear, dearly, 376, 2242.

Deeth, dethe, death, 276.

Degre, degree, (1) a step, 1032; (2) rank or station in life, 572, 576.

Deinte, deynte, deyntee, sb. a dainty, rarity; adj. rare, valuable.

Del, part, portion, whit, 967, 1233. *Never a del* = never a whit, *somdel,* somewhat.

Delen, to have dealings with.

Delit, delyt, delight, pleasure, 821.

Delve, to dig (*dolven*).

Delyvere, quick, active, nimble.

Delyverly, quickly.

Deme, demen, to judge, decide, doom, suppose, *deem,* 1023.

Departe, to part, separate, 276.

Departyng, separation, 1916.

Depeynted, painted, depicted, 1169.

Dere, dear. See `Deere.

Dere, deren, to hurt, injure, 964.

Derk, derke, dark, 1137.

Derknesse, darkness, 593.

Derre, dearer, 590.

Derreyne, 751. See *Darreyne.*

Desdeyn, disdain.

Desir, desyr, desire, 385.

Desiryng, sb. desire, 1064.

Despit, despite, despyt, malicious anger, vexation, 83.

Despitous, angry to excess, cruel, merciless, 738.

Destreine, destreyne, to vex, constrain, 597. *District* and *distress* are from the same source.

Destruie, distruye, to destroy, 472.

Deth. See *Deeth*.

Dette, a debt.

Detteles, free from debt.

Devise, devyse, (1) to direct, order; (2) to relate, describe, 136, 190.

Devise, devys, opinion, decision, direction.

Devoir, duty, 1740.

Devynynge, divination, 1663.

Devysyng, a putting in order. preparation, 1638.

Deye, a female servant.

Deye, deyen, to die, 251.

Deyere, a dyer.

Deyne, to deign.

Deynte. See *Deinte*.

Deys, dais, table of state, the high table, 1342.

Dich, a ditch. See *Dyke*.

Diete, dyete, diet, daily food.

Digestible, easy to be digested.

Digestives, things to help digestion.

Dight, prepared, dressed, 183.

Digne, worthy, proud, disdainful.

Dischevele, with hair hanging loose.

Disconfiture, disconfytyng, defeat, 150, 1861.

Disconfort, discomfort, 1152.

Disconforten, to dishearten, 1846.

Discrecioun, discretion, 921.

Discret, discreet.

Disheryt, disinherited, 2068.

Disjoint, disjoynt, a difficult situation, 2104.

Dispence, expense, expenditure, 1024.

Dispitously, angrily, cruelly, 266·

Disport, sport, diversion.

Disposicioun, control, guidance, 229.

Disputisoun, disputation.

Divisioun, distinction, 922.

Docked, cut short.

Doke, a duck.

Domb, dombe, dumb.

Dome, doom, decision. judgment, opinion. See *Deme*.

Dominacioun, power, control, 1900.

Don, doon, to do, cause, make, take, 1047.

Dong, donge, dung.

Dore, a door.

Dorste. See *Dar*.

Doseyn, a dozen.

Doughtren, daughters.

Doun, down, 132.

Doute, doubt, fear, 283.

Douteles, doubtless, without doubt, 973.

Dowves, doves, 1104.

Dragges, drugs.

Drawe, to carry, lead, 1689.

Drecched, troubled (by dreams).

Drede, dreden, to fear, dread, doubt. *To drede*, to be feared.

Dredful, cautious, timid, 621.

Dreem, dreeme, dreme, a dream.

Dreme, dremen, to dream.

Dremynges, dreams.

Drenchyng, drowning, 1598.

Dresse, to set in order, 1736.

Dreye, dry, 2166.

Dreynt (p.p. of *drenche*), drowned.

Dronke, dronken, p.p. drunk.

Dronken, pl. pret. drank.

Drope, a drop.

Drowpede, drooped.

Drugge, to drag, *drudge*, to do laborious work, 558.

Duk, a leader, duke. (2) Fr. *duc*, Lat. *dux*, from *ducere*, to lead,

Dure, to endure, last, 1912.

Dusken, pl. pres. grow dark or dim, 1948.

Dweld, p.p. dwelt, 370.

Dwelle, to tarry, 496, 803.

Dyamauntz, diamonds, 1289.

Dyapred, variegated, diversified with flourishes or sundry figures· 1300.

Dyched, diked, 1030. See *Dich, Dyke.*

Dyete. See *Diete.*

Dyke, to make *dikes* or *ditches.*

Dym, dull, indistinct, 1575.

Dys, dice, 380.

Dyvynistre, a divine, 1953.

Ecclesiaste, an ecclesiastical person.

Ech, eche, each.

Echon, echoon, each one.

Eek, ek, also, moreover, *eke.*

Eelde, elde, age, old age, 1589, 1590.

Eeres, eres, ears, 664.

Eese, ese, pleasure, amusement, ease.

Eet, et, ate, did eat, 1190.

Eft, again, after, 811. *Eft-sone, eftsones,* afterwards, presently.

Eghen, eyes. See *Eyen.*

Elde. See *Eelde.*

Elles, else.

Embrowded, embroidered.

Emforth, to the extent of, even with, 1377.

Empoysonyng, poisoning, 1602.

Emprise, an undertaking, enterprise, 1682.

Encens, incense, 1571.

Encombred, (1) wearied, tired, 860; (2) troubled, in danger. It is sometimes written *acombred.*

Encres, sb. increased, 1326.

Encresce, encrecen, to increase, 457.

Endelong, endlonge, lengthways, along, 1133, 1820.

Endere, one who causes the death of another, 1918.

Endite, to dictate, relate, 522.

Enduren, to endure.

Enfecte, tainted (by bribery).

Engendred, produced.

Engyned, tortured, racked.

Enhaunse, to raise, 576.

Enhorte, to encourage, 1993. We have *discourage* and *dishearten,* but *enhorte* has given way to *encourage,* 1993.

Enoynt, anointed, 2103.

Ensample, example.

Enspired, inspired, breathed into.

Entente, intention, purpose, 142.

Entuned, tuned, intoned.

Envyned, stored with wine.

Eny, any.

Er, ere, before, 182, 297.

Erchedeknes, archdeacon's.

Ere, to plough, *ear,* 28. *Earing* is used in our Eng. Bible.

Erly, early.

Ernest, earnest, 267, 268. A.S. *eornest,* zeal, ardor; O.Du. *ern.sten,* to endeavor.

Erst than, for *er than,* before that, 708. *Er* = before; *erst* = first.

Erthe, earth, 388.

Eschaunge, exchange.

Eschue, to avoid, shun, 2185.

Esed, entertained, accommodated.

Esely, esily, easily.

Esen, to entertain, 1336. See *Eese.*

Espye, to see, discover, 254, 562.

Est, east.

Estat, estate, state, condition.

Estatlich, estatly, stately, dignified.

Estres, the inward parts of a building, 1113.

Esy, easy, moderate.

Et, ate. See *Eet.*

Ete, eten, to eat.

Eterne, eternal, 251.

Evel, evil. **Evele,** badly, 269.

Everich, everych, every, every one, 1269.

Everichon, everychon, every one.

Everych a, every, each.

Ew, a yew-tree, 2065.

Expounede, expounded.

Ey, an egg.

Eyen, eyghen, eghen, eyes.

Eyle, to ail, 223.

Eyr, air, 388.

Fader, father; gen. sing. *fader.*

Fadme, fathoms, 2058.

Fair, fayr, faire, fayre, adj. beautiful, fair, good; adv. gracefully, neatly.

Fairnesse, (1) beauty, 240; (2) honesty of life.

Faldyng, a sort of coarse cloth.

Falle, befell.

Fals, false, 295.

Falwe, pale, 506.

Famulier, familiar, homely.

Fare, proceeding, affair, 951.

Fare, faren, to go, proceed; p.p. *Faren, fare,* pl. pres. *faren,* 403, 407, 537, 1578. A.S. *faran,* to go, pret. *fór,* p.p. *gefaren.*

Farsed, stuffed. *Farse,* to stuff.

Faste, near, 618, 830.

Faughte (O.E. *faght*), fought.

Fayn, fayne, glad, gladly.

Fedde, pret. fed.

Fee, money, reward.

Feeld, feelde, feld, a field, 28.

Feend, feende, fend, a fiend, devil.

Feer, feere, fear, 1486. See *Fer.*

Feith, faith. See *Fey.*

Fel, felle, cruel, fierce, 701, 1772. A. S. *fell,* O.Fr. *fel,* cruel, fierce;

felon, cruel; *felonie,* anger, cruelty, treason.

Felawe, a fellow. O.E. *felaghe.* The syllable *fe = fee,* goods, and *law =* order, law. Cp.O.N. *félagi,* a fellow, a sharer in goods.

Felaweschipe, fellowship.

Feld, felled, cut down, 2066.

Feld, field. See *Feeld.*

Felonie, felonye, crime, disgraceful conduct of any kind, 1138.

Fend, fende, fiend. See *Feend.*

Fer, far, 992. (Comp. *ferre,* 1202, superl. *ferrest.*

Fer, fere, fear, terror, 475.

Ferd, fered, frightened, terrified. See *Aferd.*

Ferde, (1) went, proceeded; pl. *ferden,* 789; (2) acted, conducted, 514. A.S. *féran,* to go.

Ferforth, ferforthly, far forth, as far as, 102.

Fermacye, a medicine, pharmacy, 1855.

Ferne, ancient.

Ferre, ferrer, farther.

Fers, fierce, 740.

Ferthing, farthing, fourth part; hence a very small portion of anything.

Fest, feste, a feast, 25. Lat. *festum.*

Feste, to feast, 1335.

Festne, to fasten.

Fet, fetched, brought, 1669.

Fether, a feather.

Fetously, fetysly, neatly, properly.

Fettres, fetters (for the *feet* and legs), 421.

Fetys, neat, well-made.

Fey, faith, 268.

Feyne, to feign.

Fiers, fierce, 1087.

Fil (pret. of *fallen*), fell. *Fillen*, pl. 91.

Fir, fyr, fire, 2093.

Fithele, fiddle.

Flatour, flatterer.

Fleigh (pret. of *fle*), flew.

Flessh, flesh.

Flen, to flee, flee from, 312.

Flete, to float, swim, 1539.

Fletyng, floating, 1098.

Flex, flax. A.S. *fleax*. It is probably connected with A.S. *feax*, hair.

Flikeryng, fluttering, 1104.

Flotery, wavy, flowing, 2025.

Flough, fleigh, flew.

Flour, flower, 124.

Flowen, pret. pl. flew.

Floytynge, playing on a flute.

Folk, people.

Folwe, to follow, 1509.

Fomy, foamy, foaming, 1648.

Fond, found, provided.

Foo, fo, foe, enemy. A.S. *fá*, enemy. See *Fend*.

Foom, foam, 801.

For, (1) because; (2) '*for* al,' notwithstanding, 1162.

For, for fear of.

Forbere, to forbear, 27.

Forblak, very black, 1286.

Fordo, to ruin, destroy, 702.

Forgete, to forget (p.p. *forgeten, foryeten*), 2196.

Forheed, forehead.

Forncast, pre-ordained.

Forneys, furnace. Fr. *fournaise*, It. *fornace*, Lat. *furnus*, an oven.

For-old, very old, 1284.

Forpyned, wasted away (through *pine* or torment), tormented. See *Pyne*.

Fors, force, 1865.

Forslouthe, to lose through sloth.

Forster, a forester.

Forther, further. A.S. *furthra*. The O.E. *forthere* signifies also fore, front. The root *fore* occurs in *former, foremost*.

Forthermore, furthermore, 211.

Forthren, to further, aid, 279.

Forthy, therefore.

Fortune, to make fortunate, to give good or bad fortune, 1519.

Forward, covenant, agreement.

Forwetyng, foreknowledge. See *Wite*.

Forwot, foreknows.

Foryete, forget, 1024. See *Forgete*.

Foryeve, to forgive, 960.

Fother, a load, properly a carriage-load, 1050. It is now used for a certain weight of lead.

Foughten, p.p. fought.

Foul, fowel, a bird, *fowl*, 1579.

Founden, p.p. found, 754.

Foundre, to founder, fall down, 1829.

Foyne, foynen, to make a pass in fencing, to push, *foine*, 796. 1692.

Fraknes, freckles, 1311. Cp. Ger. *Fleck, Flecken*, a spot, stain.

Fre, free, generous, willing.

Fredom, freedom, liberality.

Freend, frend, a friend, 610 'The English *friend* is a participle present. The verb *frijon*, in Gothic, means to love, hence *frijond*, a lover. It is the Sanskrit *prî*, to love.' (Max Müller.)

Frendly, frendlych, friendly, 794, 1822.

Frendschipe, friendship.

Frere, a friar.

Fresch, fressh, fressche, fresh, 1318. A.S. *fersc*, O.N. *friskr*. The Eng. *frisk, frisky*, are from the same source.

Frete, freten, to eat (p.p. *freten*), 1161. Eng. *fret*.

Fro, froo, from. It still exists in the phrase 'to and *fro*.'

Frothen, to froth, foam, 801.

Fulfild, filled full, 82.

Fume, effects of gluttony or drunkenness. Hence the use of *fume* in the sense of 'the vapors, dumps.'

Fumetere, name of a plant, *fumitory.*

Fyled, cut, formed, 1294.

Fyn, fine, 614.

Fynde, to invent, provide.

Fyr, fire, 2084. *Fyry,* fiery, 706.

Fyr-reed, red as fire.

Gabbe, to lie.

Gadere, gadre, to gather.

Galyngale, sweet cyperus.

Game, pleasure, sport, 948. A.S. *gamen.*

Gamede, verb. impers. pleased.

Gan (a contraction of *began*), is used as a mood auxiliary, e.g. *gan espye* = did see, 254; began, 682.

Gappe, a gap, 781.

Gapyng, having the mouth wide open, gaping, 1150, to stare; Eng. *gulp.*

Garget, the throat. Fr. *gorge,* a throat.

Garleek, garlick; the spear-plant, from A.S. *gar,* a spear, *leac,* an herb, plant, *leek.* We have the second element in other names of plants, as *hemlock, charlock, barley.*

Gaste, to terrify. See *Agast.*

Gastly, horrible, 1126. See *Agast.*

Gat, got, obtained.

Gattothed (having teeth far apart), lascivious. Du. *gat,* a hole. It is sometimes written *gaptothed,* and *gagtoothed* = having projecting teeth, which also signifies lascivious.

Gaude grene, a light green color, 1221.

Gayler, a jailer, 206.

Gayne, to avail, 318.

Gaytres beryis, berries of the dogwood-tree.

Geere, manner, habit, 514, 673. See *Gere.*

Gees, geese.

Geet, jet. Fr. *jaiet,* Lat. *gagates.* Used for beads, and held in high estimation.

Gentil, noble.

Gentilesse, gentleness.

Gepoun, gypoun, a short cassock, 1262.

Ger, gear, 1322. See *Gere.*

Gere, gear, all sorts of instruments, tools, utensils, armor, apparel, fashion, 158.

Gerful, changeable, 680. See *Gery.*

Gerland, a garland, 196.

Gerner, a garner.

Gery, changeable, 678.

Gesse, to deem, suppose, think, *guess.*

Get, fashion, mode.

Gete, to get, obtain.

Giggyng, clattering, 1646.

Gile, guile, 1738. O.Fr. *guille,* deceit, of the same origin as Eng. *wile, wily.*

Gilteles, free from guilt, guiltless, 454.

Gipser, a pouch or purse.

Gird, p.p. girded, girt.

Girdel, gurdel, girdle.

Girt, pierced, 152. *Thurgh-girt,* pierced through, is used also by Surrey.

Gise, fashion, way.

Gladen, to console, gladden, 1979.

Gladere, sb. one who makes glad, 1365; adj. more glad, 2193.

Glaryng, staring (like the eyes of the hare).

Gleed, gleede, a live coal, *gleed*, 1139. A.S. *gléd*, O.Du *gloed*. Cp. O.N. *glóa*, to burn. *glow; glod*, a live coal; Ger. *glühen*, to glow; *gluth*, hot coals.

Gliteren, to glitter, shine, 2032. O.N. *glitra*, to glitter.

Glowen, to glow, shine; *Gloweden* (pl. pret.), shone, 1274; *Glowyng*, fiery. See *Gleed*.

Go, gon, goo, goon (p.p. *go, gon, goon*), to go, walk, *Goth.* goes, 598. *Goon* (pl.), go, walk.

Gobet, piece, morsel, fragment. Prov. Eng. *gob*, Gael. *gob*, the mouth; whence *gobble, gabble,* etc.

Godhede, godhead, divinity, 1523.

Golyardeys, a buffoon. See note, p. 138.

Gon, to go. See *Go*.

Gonne (pl. of *gan*), began, did, 800.

Good, property, goods.

Goost, ghost, spirit.

Goot, a goat.

Gooth, goes, 213.

Goune, gowne, a gown. It. *gonna*, Mid. Lat. *guna, gouna*.

Governaunce, management, control, management of affairs, business matters, 455.

Governynge, control.

Graunte, grant, permission, 448.

Graunte, to grant, consent to.

Grauntyng, consent, permission, 1581.

Gree, the prize, *grant*, 1875.

Greece, grease.

Greene, grene, green.

Greet, gret (def. form and pl. *greete, grete*), great (comp. *gretter*, superl. *gretteste*), 5, 218, 559.

Greve, to grieve. *Agreved*, 1199.

Greve, a grove, 63. This form is used by some of the Elizabethan poets.

Greyn, grain.

Griffoun, a griffin, 1275.

Grim, grym, fierce, 1661. A.S. *grimm*, fierce, furious.

Grisly, horrible, dreadful, 505.

Grone, gronen, to groan; *Gronyng*, groaning.

Grope, to try, test. It signifies originally to feel with the hands, to *grope*. Cp. *grabble, grip, grasp*, etc.

Grote, a groat.

Groynyng, stabbing, 1602.

Grucchen, to murmur, grumble, *grudge*, 2187.

Gruf, with face flat to the ground, 91; whence Eng. *grovelling, grovel*.

Grys, fur of the gray rabbit.

Gulde, or **Golde,** a flower commonly called a *turnsol*, 1071. Fr. *goude*, a *marigold*, so called from its golden color.

Gult, gylt, guilt, conduct which has to be atoned for by a payment. A.S. *gild*, a money payment; Swiss *gult*, Dan. *gjeld*, a a debt. Cp. A.S. *gildan*, Ger. *gelten*, to pay, *yield*.

Gulty, guilty.

Gurles, young people, either male or female. Low Ger. *gör, göre*, a child. The O.E. *wench-el*, a boy, is our word *wench*.

Gye, to guide, 1092. Fr. *guider, guier*.

Gylt, guilt, 907. See *Gult*.

Gynglen, to jingle.

Gynne, to begin, 2160.

Gyse, guise, fashion, mode, *wise*, 135, 350. Fr. *guise*, Welsh *gwis*, Ger. *Weise*, Eng. *wise*, mode, fashion.

Haberdasshere, a seller of hats. 'The *Haberdasher* heapeth wealth by *hattes.*' Gascoigne, The Fruites of Warre.

Habergeon, habergoun, a diminutive *hauberk*, a small coat of mail, 1261. O.Fr. *hauberc*, O.H.Ger. *halsberc*, A.S. *healsbeorg*, a coat of mail, from *heals*, the neck, and *beorgan*, to cover or protect.

Hade = O.E. *havede* (sing.), had.

Hakke, to hack, 2007. Du. *hacken*, Ger. *hacken*, to cut up, chop; Dan. *hakke*, to peck; Fr. *hacher*, to mince; whence Eng. *hash*, *hatch*, *hatchet*.

Halwes, saints. A.S. *bálga*, a saint (as in "All Hallows" E'en), from *hál*, whole.

Hamer, a hammer, 1650.

Han = *haven*, to have.

Happe, to happen, befall. Whence *happy*, mis-*hap*, per*haps*, may-hap. O.E. *happen*, happy; O.N. *happ*, fortune; W. *hap*, luck.

Hardily, certainly.

Hardynesse, boldness, 1090.

Haried, harried, taken as prisoner. Fr. *harier*, to hurry, harass, molest. (Cotgrave.)

Harlot. It signifies (1) a young person; (2) a person of low birth; (3) a person given to low conduct; (4) a ribald.

Harlotries, ribaldries.

Harnays, harneys, herneys, armor, gear, furniture, *harness*, 148, 755.

Harneysed, equipped.

Harre, a hinge.

Harrow, a cry of distress. O.Fr. *harau, hare!* Scottish *harro*, a cry for help.

Hauberk, a coat of mail, 1573. See *Habergeon*.

Haunt, (1) a district, (2) custom, practice, skill.

Hede, heed, heede, head.

Heeld, held.

Heep, heap, assembly, host.

Heer, heere, here, hair.

Heere, to hear.

Heete, to promise, 1540.

Heeth, heethe, a heath.

Hegge, a hedge.

Heigh, heygh, heih, high, 207; great, 940.

Heigher, upper.

Hele, health, 413.

Helpen of, to help off, get rid of.

Hem, them.

Hemself, themselves, 396.

Hemselve, hemselven, themselves.

Heng (pret. of *honge*), hanged.

Henne, hence, 1498.

Hente, henten, seize, take hold of, get, 46. (Pret. *hente*, 442; p.p. *hent*, 723.) A.S. *hentan*.

Her, here, 933.

Heraude, a herald, 159, 1675. Fr. *hérauld, héraut*, from O.H. Ger. *haren*, to shout.

Herbergage, herbergh, lodging, inn, port, harbor.

Herd, haired, 1660.

Herde, a herd, keeper of cattle, a shep*herd*, 603.

Here, heer, hair, 1285. See *Heer*.

Here, their, of them, 320. *Here aller* = of them all.

Herknen, to hark, hearken, listen, 668, 985, 1674.

Herneys, 148. See *Harnays*.

Hert, a hart, 831.

Herte, a heart.

Herte-spon, 1748. The provincial *heart-spoon* signifies the navel.

Herteles, without heart, cowardly.

Hertely, heartily.

Hest, command, *behest*, 1674. A.S. *hœs*, from *hátan*, to command.

Hethe, heath. See *Heeth.*

Hethene, a heathen.

Hethenesse, the country inhabited by the heathens, in contra-distinction to *Christendom.*

Heve, to heave, raise. *Heve of =* to lift off.

Hevenlyche, heavenly, 197.

Hew, hewe, color, complexion, *hue*, 506. *Hewes*, colors for painting, 1230.

Hewe, to cut, 564.

Hewed, colored. See *Hew.*

Hey, heye, heygh, heyh, high, highly.

Hider, hither.

Hidous, hideous, 1120. *Hidously.* hideously, 843.

Hight, highte, was called, promised, 333, 1614.

Highte. ' *On highte* ' = aloud, 926.

Hih, hihe, high, 1605.

Hiled, hidden, kept secret.

Himselve, himselven, dat. and acc. of *himself.*

Hipes, hips.

Hire, her.

Hit, it.

Ho, hoo, an interjection commanding a cessation of anything, 848, 1675. Cp. the carter's *whoa!* to his horse to stop.

Hold, ' in hold,' in possession, custody.

Holde, holden, beholden, 449; esteemed, held, 832, 1861.

Holly, wholly. See *Hool.*

Holpen, helped. See *Helpen.*

Holt, holte, a wood, grove.

Holwe, hollow, a hole, a ditch. The termination -*we* or -*ow* had originally a diminutival force.

Hom, home; *Homward*, homeward, 1881, 2098.

Homicides, murderers.

Hond, honde, hand.

Honest, creditable, honorable, becoming.

Honge, hongen, to hang (pret. *heng*), 638, 1552.

Honte, honter, a hunter, 780, 820.

Honte, honten, to hunt, 782. *On hontyng =* a-hunting, 829.

Hoo. See *Ho.*

Hool, hoole, whole. A.S. *hál*, whole, sound; whence *wholesome, holy,* etc.

Hoom, home. *Hoomly*, homely.

Hoost, host.

Hoot, hoote, hote, hot, hotly.

Hoppesteres (applied to ships), warlike, 1159. -*ster* is a termination marking the feminine gender, as in modern Eng. *spinster.*

Hors, horse. Pl. *hors*, horses, 1634.

Hostelrie, hostelrye, an hotel, inn.

Hostiler, innkeeper.

Hote, hot. See *Hoot.*

Hote, to be called, 699. See *Heete, Hight.*

Hous, hows, house. *Houshaldere*, householder.

Housbondry, economy.

Howpede, = *houped*, whooped. *Hooping-cough* is properly *whooping-cough.*

Humblesse, humility, 923.

Hunte, a hunter, 1160.

Hunteresse, a female hunter, 1489.

Hurtle, to push, 1758.

Hust, hushed, 2123.

Hye, hyhe, high, highly, 39, 1217.

Hye, haste, 2121; to hasten, 1416. *In hye =* in haste, hastily.

Hyndreste, hindmost. Cp. *overest*, overmost, uppermost.

Hyne, hind, servant.

Hynge (pl. pret. of *hongen*),hung.

I, a prefix used to denote the past participle (like the modern German *ge*), as in the following words:—*I-bete*, ornamented, 121; *I-born*, born, 161; *I-bounde*, bound, 1293; *I-bounden*, bound, 291; *I-brought*, brought; *I-caught*, caught, 1093; *I-cleped*, called, 9; *I-clenched*, fastened, clinched, 1133; *I-doo*, *I-doon*, done, 167, 1676; *I-drawe*, drawn, 1784; *I-fetered*, fettered, 371; *I-laft*, left, 1888; *I-mad*, *I-maad*, *I-maked*, made, 1207, 2236; clotted, 1307; *I-sent*, sent, 2012; *I-set*, set, appointed, 777; *I-skalded*, scalded, 1162; *I-slawe*, *I-slayn*, slain, 85; *I-styked*, pierced, stabbed, 707; *I-swore*, sworn, 274; *I-wedded*, wedded, 2240; *I-wrye*, covered, 2046.

Iliche, iliche, alike, 681, 1668.

Ilke, same. Cp. " of that *ilk*."

In, inne, house, lodging,inn,1579.

Inequal, unequal, 1413.

Inne, adv. in, 760.

Inned, lodged, entertained, 1334.

Inough, enough.

Iwis, iwys, indeed, truly. (It is often contracted to *wis*.)

Jalous, jealous, 471.

Jangle, to prate, babble.

Jangler, a prater, babbler.

Jape, a trick, jest.

Jape, to befool, deceive, 871. It is probably connected with Eng. *gabble, gabbe,* etc.

Jolitee, joyfulness, 949.

Jolyf, joyful, pleasant. *Jolynesse,* joyfulness.

Journee, a day's journey, 1880.

Juge; jugge, a judge, 854.

Juggement, judgment.

Juste, jousten, to joust, tilt, engage in a tournament, 1628.

Justes, =*jouste,* a tournament, 1802.

Juwyse, judgment, 881.

Kaytives, prisoners, wretches, 859. See *Caitif.*

Keep, keepe, kepe, care, attention, heed. *Take keep =* take care, 531.

Keepe, kepe (pret. *kepte,* p.p. *kep*), to guard, preserve, take care (as in *I kepe nat =* I care not), 1380.

Kembd, combed, neatly trimmed, 1285.

Kempe, shaggy, literally crooked, 1276.

Kene, keen, sharp.

Kervere, a carver, 1041.

Kervyng, cutting, carving, 1057. See *Carf.*

Keverchef, a kerchief.

Kind, kynd, kynde, nature, 1593.

Knarre, a knotted, thick-set fellow.

Knarry, full of *gnarrs* or knots, 1119.

Knave, a boy, a servant, 1870.

Knighthede, knighthood, 1931.

Knobbe, a pimple.

Knowe, pp. known , 345, 1442.

Knyf, a knife, 1141.

Kouthe, known, renowned. See *Couthe.*

Kyn, kine.

Kyndled, lighted, 1437.

Kynrede, kindred, 428.

Laas, las, a lace, belt, 1093.

Laas, net, snare, 959.

Lacert, a fleshy muscle, so called from being shaped like a lizard, 1895.

Lad (p.p.), 1762; *Ladde* (pret.), 588; led, carried.

Lafte (pret. sing.); *Laften* (pret. pl.), 34, left, ceased. Cp. the phrase " *left* off."

Lak, want, lack.

Lakke, to lack, be wanting, 1422.

Langage, language.

Large, adj. free; adv. largely. Chaucer says, "at his *large*," 425, where we should say "at large."

Las, snare. See *Laas*.

Lasse, less, 898.

Lasyng, lacing, fastening, 1646. See *Laas*.

Lat. imp. let, *lat be*, cease.

Late, lately, recently.

Latoun, a kind of brass, or tinned iron. *latten*.

Launde, a plain surrounded by trees, hunting-grounds, 833. It seems to be, with a difference of meaning, our modern word *lawn*.

Laurer, a laurel, 169. "In a fayre fresh and grene *laurere*."

Lawghe, to laugh.

Laxatif, laxatyf, a purging medicine.

Laynere, a lanner or whiplash, 1646.

Lazar, lazer, a leper.

Lechecraft, the skill of a physician, 1887.

Leede (dat.), a caldron, copper. It also signifies a kettle.

Leef (pl. *leves, leeves*), leaf, 980.

Leef (def. form voc. case *leeve*), dear, beloved, pleasing, 278. 979.

Leeme, gleam.

Leep, leaped, 1829.

Leere, lere, to learn.

Leese, lese, to lose, 432.

Leesyng, loss. 849.

Leet (pret.), let, 343.

Leeve, believe, 2230.

Lef, imp. leave, 756.

Lene, to lend, give, 2224.

Lene, leene, lean, poor.

Lenger. lengere, longer.

Lepart. a leopard, 1328.

Lere. See *Leere*.

Lerne, to learn.

Lese. to lose, 357. See *Leese*.

Lest, leste, least, 263.

Leste, list, lust, pleasure, delight, joy, 493.

Leste, liste, lyste, luste, vb. impers. please, 194.

Lesynges, leasing, lies, 1069.

Lete, lette, to leave, 477. "*Letten of*" = refrain from, 459. See *Leet*.

Lette, to hinder, delay, tarry, put off (pret. *lette*), 31, 1034. Cp. Eng. *late, lazy*.

Lette, delay, hindrance. See previous word.

Lever, rather (comp. of *leef* or *lief*).

Lewed, lewd, ignorant, unlearned. *Lewed-man*, a layman.

Leye, to lay.

Leyser, leisure, 330.

Licenciat, one licensed by the Pope to hear confessions in all places, and to administer penance independently of the local ordinaries.

Liche-wake, the vigil, *watch*, or *wake* held over the body of the dead, 2100.

Licour, liquor.

Liefe, beloved. See *Leef*.

Lif, lyf, life, 1918.

Ligge, to lie, 1347.

Lightly, (1) easily, (2) joyfully.

Lik, lyk, like, 443.

Like, vb. impers. to please.

Lipsede, lisped.

Liste. See *Leste*.

Listes, lystes, lists, a place enclosed for combats or tournaments. 1687.

Litarge, white lead.

Lite, lyte, litel, little, 476.

Lith. lies, 360.

Lith, a limb, any member of the body.

Live, dat. of *lif*, life; *on live*, in life, alive, 1840.

Lodemenage, pilotage.

Logge, loge, to lodge, sb. a lodging, inn. *Loggyng*, lodging.

Loken, to see, look upon, 925.

Loken, locked, enclosed.

Lokkes, locks (of hair), curls.

Lokyng, appearance, sight, 1313.

Lond, londe, land.

Longe, longen, to belong, 1420.

Longe, longen, to desire, long for.

Longes, lungs, 1894.

Loode, a load, 2060.

Loodesterre, a loadstar, the pole-star, 1201. The first element is the A.S. *lád*, away, from *lœdan*, to lead, conduct. It occurs again in *loadstone; lode*, a vein of metal ore.

Loor, loore, lore, precept, doctrine, learning. See *Leere*.

Lordynges, lordlings (a diminutive of *lord*), sirs, my masters.

Lorn, lost. See *Leese*.

Los, loss, 1685.

Losengour, a flatterer, liar.

Losten (pl. pret.), lost. See *Leese*.

Loth, odious, hateful, disagreeable, *loath*, unwilling, 979.

Lovyere, a lover.

Lowde, loud, loudly.

Luce, a pike.

Lust, pleaseth. See *Leste*.

Lust, pleasure.

Luste, pleased.

Lusty, pleasant, joyful, 655. *Lustily, Lustely*, merrily, joyfully, 671.

Lustynesse, pleasure, 1081.

Lyf, life.

Lyfly, lifelike, 1229.

Lyggen, to lie, 3 pl. pres.

Lyk, like, alike.

Lymes, limbs, 1277.

Lymytour, a friar licensed to ask alms within a certain limit.

Lyn, pl. lie.

Lynage, lyne, lineage, 252, 693.

Lynd, linden-tree, 2064.

Lystes. See *Listes*.

Lyt, lyte, little, 335.

Lyve. See *Live*.

Lyvere, livery.

Lyves, alive, living, 1537.

Maad, mad, p.p. made.

Maat, dejected, downcast, 98.

Maist, mayest, 385. *Maistow*, mayest thou, 378.

Maister, mayster, a master, chief, a skilful artist *Maister-streete* = the chief street, 2044.

Maistre, skill, power, superiority.

Make, a companion or *mate*, 1698.

Maked, p.p. made, 1666.

Male, a portmanteau, bag, *mail*.

Malencolie, malencolye, sb. melancholy. Adj. *Malencolyk* 517.

Manace, manasyng, a threat, menace, 1145, 1178.

Mancioun, a mansion, 1116.

Maner, manere, manner, kind, sort, 1017. " A *maner* dey " = a sort of dey, or farm-servant.

Manhede, manhood, manliness.

Mantelet, a little mantle, a short mantle, 1305.

Manye, mania, madness, 516.

Many oon, many a one.

Marchaunt, a merchant.

Marschal, marshal of the hall. " The *marshal of the hall* was the person who, at public festivals, placed every person according to his rank. The *marshal of the field* presided over any outdoor games.

Martirdam, torment, martyrdom, 602.

Martyre, to torment, 704.

Mary, marrow.

Mase, a wild fancy. Cp. the phrase " to be in a *maze*."

Mateere, mater, matere, matter, 401.

Matrimoyn, matrimony, 2237.

Maugre, mawgre, in spite of, 311, 1760.

Maunciple, an officer who has the care of purchasing victuals for an Inn of Court or College.

Maydenhode, maidenhood, 1471.

Mayntene, maynteyne, to maintain, 583.

Mayst, mayest. See *Maist.*

Med, meed, mede, meede, a reward, *meed.*

Mede, a mead or meadow, hayland.

Medlé, of a mixed color. Fr. *medler, mesler,* to mix.

Meel, a meal. A.S. *mœl,* what is marked out, a separate part, a meal, a mark, spot.

Meke, meek.

Mellere, a miller.

Men, one; used like the Fr. *on.*

Mencioun, mention, 35.

Mene, to mean, intend (pret. *mente*).

Menstralcye, minstrelsy, 1666.

Mere, a mare.

Merie, mery, merye, murye, pleasant, joyful, merry, 641.

Meriely, pleasantly.

Mermayde, a mermaid.

Mertha, myrthe, pleasure, amusement.

Mervaille, mervaylle, marvel.

Meschaunce, mischance, misfortune, 1151.

Mescheef, meschief, misfortune, what turns out ill, 468. Fr. *meschef (mes = minus,* less; *chef = caput,* head).

Messager, a messenger, 633.

Mester, trade, business, occupation; *mester men =* sort of men, 852.

Mesurable, moderate.

Met, p.p. dreamed. See *Mete,* 666.

Mete, meat, food. Eng. *mess.*

Mete, to meet, 666.

Mete, to dream, pret. *mette.* It is used impersonally as *me mette,* I dreamed.

Meth, mead, a drink made of honey, 1421.

Mewe, a *mue* or coop where fowls were fattened.

Meyné, household, attendants, suite, domestics, 400.

Middel, middle, midst.

Minister, mynistre, an office of justice. "*Minister* meant etymologically a small man; and it was used in opposition to *magister,* a big man. *Minister* is connected with *minus,* less; *magister* with *magis,* more. (Max Müller, Science of Language.)

Misboden, insulted, injured, 51.

Mischaunce. See *Meschaunce.*

Mo, moo, more. A.S. *má.*

Moche, mochel, muchel, adj. much, great; adv. greatly. *Moche and lite =* great and small.

Moder, mother.

Moevere, mover, first cause, 2129.

Mone, moone, the moon.

Moneth, a month.

Mood, anger, 902.

Moone, a moan, lamentation, 508.

Moorning, mourning, 2110.

Moot, may, must, ought (pl. pres. *mooten,* pret. *moste, muste*).

Mor, more, greater, more, 898.

Mordre, sb. murder.

Mordrer, a murderer.

Mormal, a cancer, sore, or gangrene,

Morne, adj. morning.

Morthre, vb. to murder; sb. murder, 398.

Mortreux, a kind of soup or pottage.

Morwe, morwenynge, morning, morrow, 204.

Mosel, Fr. *museau*, muzzle, nose of an animal, 1293.

Most, greatest, most, 37.

Moste, must. See *Moot*.

Mot, may, must. See *Moot*.

Mote, pl. must.

Motteleye, motley.

Mountaunce, amount, value, 712.

Mous, a mouse, 403.

Mowe, be able, 2141.

Murmure, murmuring, 1601.

Murtheryng, murdering. 1143.

Murye, pleasant, merry, 528.

Mynde, a remembrance, 544, 1048.

Mynour, a miner, 1607.

Mynstralcye, minstrelsy, 1339.

Myrour, a mirror, 541.

Myselven, myself.

Myshappe, to mishap, turn out badly, befall amiss, 788.

Myster, need, necessity, 482.

Nacioun, nation.

Naker, a kettle-drum, 1653.

Nam' = *ne* + *am*, am not, 264.

Namelyche, especially, 410.

Narwe, close, narrow.

Nas = *ne* + *was*, was not.

Nat, not.

Nath = *ne* + *hath*, hath not, 65.

Natheles, nevertheless.

Ne, adv. not; conj. nor. *Ne . . . ne* = neither . . . nor. *Ne . . . but*, only.

Nedeth, must of necessity (die), 2170.

Neede, needful.

Needely, of necessity.

Needes, nedes, of necessity, 311. *Needes-cost* = *needes-ways*, of necessity, 619.

Neer, ner, near, nearer, 581, 992.

Neet, neat, cattle.

Neigh, neighe, neih, neyh, nigh, near, nearly, 472; *as neigh as* = as near (close) as.

Nekke, neck. *Nekke-boon*, bone of the neck.

Ner, nearer.

Nercotyks, narcotics, 614.

Nere = *ne* + *were*, were not, 17.

Newe, newly, recently.

Nexte, nearest, 555.

Nice, nyce, foolish.

Night, pl. nights.

Nightertale, the night-time; *-tale* = reckoning, period.

Nis, nys, = *ne* + *is*, is not, 43.

Noght, not.

Nolde = *ne* + *wolde*, would not.

Nombre, number.

Nomoo, no more.

Non, noon, none.

Nones, nonce.

Nonne, a nun.

Noot, not = *ne* + *wot*, know not, knows not, 181, 482. See *Wost*.

Noote, a note (in music).

Norice, nurse.

Norisching, norischynge, nutriment, nurture, 2159.

Nose-thurles, nostrils. See *Thirle*.

Not = *ne* + *wot*, knows not, 405.

Notabilite, a thing worthy to be known.

Not-heed, a crop-head.

Nother, neither, nor, 513.

Nothing, adv. not at all, 647.

Nought, not. A.S. *nawiht* = *ne* + *a* + *whit*, not a whit.

Nouthe = *nou* + *the* = now + then, just now, at present. *As nouthe* = at present.

Nygard, a niggard.

O, one, 354.

Obeissance, obeisaunce, obedience, 2116.

Observaunce, respect, 187, 642.

Of, off, 1818.

Offende, to hurt, injure, attack, 51.

Offensioun, offence, hurt, damage, 1558.

Offertorie, a sentence of Scripture said or sung after the Nicene Creed in the Liturgy of the Western Church.

Offryng, the alms collected at the Offertory.

Ofte sithes, oftentimes.

Oghte, ought.

Ok, ook, an oak, 1432, 2159.

On, oo, oon, one. *Oones*, once.

On and oon, one by one.

Ony, any.

Oonely, oonly, 515.

Opye, opium, 614.

Or, ere, before, 771. So Ps. xc. 2. " *Or ever*" = ere ever.

Or . . or = either . . or. 627, 628.

Oratorye, a closet set apart for prayers or study, 1047.

Ordeyne, to ordain, 1695.

Ordynaunce, plan, orderly disposition, 1709.

Orisoun, prayer, orison, 1514.

Orlogge, a clock.

Oth, an oath.

Oughne, own.

Outehees, outcry, alarm, 1154.

Outrely, utterly, wholly.

Out-sterte, started out.

Over, upper. *Overeste*, uppermost.

Overal, everywhere. Cp. Ger. *überall*.

Overlippe, upper lip.

Over-ryden, ridden over, 1164.

Overspradde, pret. spread over.

Over-thwart, athwart, across,

1133. (Eng. *queer* = O.E. *quer*, Ger. *quer*, athwart.)

Owen, owne, own, 2219.

Owher, anywhere.

Oynement, ointment, unguent.

Oynouns, onions.

Paas, pas, a foot-pace, 1032. Fr. *pas*, Lat. *passus*.

Pace, to pass, 2140; pass on, or away, 744.

Pacient, patient.

Paleys, palace, 1341. " A palace is now the abode of a royal family. But if we look at the history of the name we are soon carried back to the shepherds of the Seven Hills. There on the Tiber, one of the seven hills was called the *Collis Palatinus*, and the hill was called *Palatinus* from *Pales*, a pastoral deity, whose festival was celebrated every year on the 21st of April, as the birthday of Rome. It was to commemorate the day on which Romulus, the wolf-child, was supposed to have drawn the first furrow on the foot of that hill, and thus to have laid the foundation of the most ancient part of Rome, the *Roma Quadrata*. On this hill, the Collis Palatinus, stood in later times the houses of Cicero and of his neighbor and enemy Catiline. Augustus built his mansion on the same hill, and his example was followed by Tiberius and Nero. Under Nero, all private houses had to be pulled down on the Collis Palatinus, in order to make room for the emperor's residence, the *Domus Aurea*, as it was called, the Golden House. This house of Nero's was henceforth called the *Palatium*, and it became the type of all the *palaces* of the kings and emperors of Europe." (Max Müller, Science of Language.)

Palfrey, a horse for the road.

Pan, the skull, brain-pan, 307.

Paramentz, ornamental furniture or clothes, 1648.

Paramour, by way of love, 297; a lover, of either sex, 1254.

Parde, pardee = *par Dieu,* a common oath.

Pardoner, a seller of indulgences.

Parfight, perfect.

Parischen, a parishioner.

Parte, party, company, 1724.

Partrich, a partridge.

Party, partly, 195. *Partye,* a part, party, 2150; adj. partial, 1799.

Pas, foot-pace. See *Paas.*

Passe, to surpass. *Passant, Passyng,* surpassing, 1249, 2027.

Payen, pagan, 1512.

Peere, equal, as in *peerless.*

Pees, peace, 589.

Peire, pair.

Pekke, pike, to pick. A.S. *pycan,* to pick, pull; Du. *picken,* to pick.

Penaunce, penance, pain, sorrow, 457.

Perce, to pierce.

Perfight, perfyt, perfect.

Perrye, jewelry, 2078.

Pers, of a sky-blue color.

Persoun, a parson or parish priest.

Pertourben, to disturb, 48.

Pestilens, pestilence, plague.

Peyne, sb. pain, grief, 439.

Peyne, peynen, to take pains, endeavor.

Peynte, to paint, 1076.

Peyre, a pair, 1263.

Pight = *pighte,* pitched, 1831.

Piked, adj. trimmed.

Pikepurs, a pick-purse, 1140.

Piled, stripped of hair, bald.

Piler, a pillar, 1135.

Pilour, a plunderer, 149. See *Piled.*

Pilwe beer, a pillow-case.

Pitaunce, a mess of victuals; properly an additional allowance served to the inmates of religious houses at a high festival.

Pitous, compassionate, piteous.

Pitously, piteously, 259.

Plat, plain, flat, 987.

Plein, pleyne, pleinly, full, fully, openly. *Pleyn, bataile =* open battle, 130.

Pleinly, pleynly, fully, 875.

Plentevous, plentiful.

Plesance, plesaunce, pleasure, 713.

Plesant, plesaunt, pleasant.

Plese, to please.

Pley, pleye, play, pleasure, 267.

Pleye, pleyen, to play, take one's pleasure. *Pleyynge,* playing, amusement. 203.

Pleyn, plain.

Pleyne, to complain, 462.

Pleynen, to complain, 393.

Pocock, peacock. It is also written *pacock.*

Pollax, a halberd, pole-axe, 1686.

Pomel, top of the head, 1831.

Pomely, marked with round spots like an apple, dappled.

Poplexie, apoplexy.

Poraille, the poor.

Pore. See *Poure.*

Port, carriage, behavior.

Portreiture, pourtreiture, a picture, 1110.

Portreying, painting, 1080.

Portreyour, a painter, 1041.

Pose, to propose, question, 304.

Post, pillar, support.

Poudre-marchaunt, a kind of spice.

Poure, poor. *Povrely*, poorly, 554.

Powpe, to make a noise with a horn.

Powre, to pore, to look close and long.

Poynaunt, pungent.

Poynt, particle, particular, 643.

Practisour, practitioner.

Preche, to preach.

Preest, prest, a priest.

Preisen, praysen, to praise.

Prese, to press, 1672.

Prest, ready. Lat. *praesto*, in readiness.

Preve, sb. *proof*, vb. to prove, put to proof.

Preye, to pray, 625.

Preyeres, prayers.

Pricasour, a hard rider.

Prik, prikke, a point, 1748.

Prike, (1) to prick, wound; (2) to spur a horse, to ride hard; (3) to excite, spur on, 185, 1820.

Prikyng, riding.

Prime, pryme, the first quarter of the artificial day, 1331.

Pris, prys, price, praise, estimation, prize, 1383. See *Preisen*.

Prively, privyly, secretly.

Propre, peculiar, own.

Prow, advantage, profit.

Prys, price, prize, fame. See *Preisen*.

Pryvyte, privity, privacy, private business, 553.

Pulle, to pluck. *Pulle a fynch* = pluck a pigeon.

Pulled, moulting.

Pultrie, poultry. Fr. *poule*, a hen; Lat. *pullus*, young of an animal.

Purchas, anything acquired (honestly or dishonestly); proceeds of begging.

Purchasour, prosecutor.

Purchasyng, prosecution.

Pure, mere, very, 421.

Purfiled, embroidered, fringed. It. *porfilo*, a border in armory, a worked edge) a *profile*.

Purpos, purpose, design, 1684.

Purs, purse. Fr. *bourse*, Lat. *bursa*, hide, skin.

Purtreiture, painting, picture, 1057.

Purtreye, portray.

Purveiaunce, purveyans, foresight, providence, plan, 394, 807, 2153.

Pynche, to find fault with.

Pyne, sb. torment, pain, grief.

Pyne, pynen, to torment, grieve, 888.

Pynoun, a pennant or ensign (borne at the end of a lance), 120.

Qualme, sickness, pestilence, 1156.

Quelle, to kill. See *Qualme*.

Quen, a queen, 24.

Queynt, pp.; pret. *queynte*, quenched, 1463, 1476. Cp. *dreynte* = drenched.

Queynte, strange, quaint, uncouth, 673, 1471.

Quod, quoth, 49, 376.

Quook, quok, quaked, trembled, 718, 904. To this family of words belong *quag, quaver, wag, wave*.

Quyke, alive, quick, 157; vb. to revive, 1477. Cp. "the *quick* and the dead."

Quyte, free, as in our phrase "to get *quit* of," hence to requite.

Quyte, to set free, 174.

Quytly, free, at liberty, 934.

Rad (p.p. of *rede*, to read), read, 1737.

Rage, vb. to play, toy wantonly; sb. a raging wind, 1127.

Ransake, to search (for plunder), ransack, 147.

Rasour, a razor, 1559.

Rather, sooner, 295. Milton uses *rathe* in the sense of "early."

Raughte (pret. of *reche*), reached, 2057.

Raunsoun, ransom, 166, 318. Lat. *red-emptio*, a purchase back, *redemption*.

Real, rial, ryal, royal, kingly; *Really*, royally, 160, 855.

Rebel, rebellious, 2188. *Rebellyng*, rebellion, 1601.

Recche, Rekke (pret. *roghte*, *roughte*), to care, take heed to, *reck*, 540, 1387, 1399.

Reccheles, reckless, careless.

Reconforte, to comfort, 1994.

Recorde, to remember, remind.

Red (imp. of *rede*), read.

Rede, reed, counsel, adviser.

Rede, to advise, explain, interpret, 2213.

Rede, to read.

Redoutyng, reverence, 1192.

Redy, ready.

Reed, plan, 358. See *Rede*.

Reed, reede, red.

Reeve, steward, bailiff. In composition, *shire-reeve* = *sheriff*.

Refreissche, to refresh, 1764.

Regne, a kingdom, reign, 8, 766.

Reherce, to rehearse. Fr. *rehercer*, to go over again, like a harrow (Fr. *herce*) over a ploughed field.

Rehersyng, rehearsal, 792.

Reken, rekne, to reckon, 1075.

Rekkenynge, reckoning.

Reme (pl. *remes*), realm.

Romenant, remenaunt, a remnant.

Rendyng, tearing (of hair), 1976.

Renges, ranks, 1736.

Renne, to run. We have this form in *rennet*, or *runnet*, that which makes milk *run* or curdle.

Rennyng, running.

Rente, revenue, income, profits.

Repentaunce, penitence, 918.

Repentaunt, penitent.

Repplicacion, a reply, 288.

Reportour, reporter.

Rescous, rescue, 1785.

Rese, to quake, shake, 1128.

Resons, opinions, reasons.

Resoun, reason, right.

Resowne, to resound, 420.

Respite, delay, 90.

Rethor, a rhetorician.

Rette, to ascribe, impute. See *Aretted*.

Reule, sb. rule, vb. to rule, 814.

Revel, feasting, merry-making, 1859.

Reverence, respect.

Revers, reverse, contrary.

Rewe, rewen, to be sorry for, to have compassion or pity on, to *rue*, 1005, 1375.

Rewe, a row, line, 2008.

Rewfulleste, most sorrowful, 2028.

Rewle, to rule. See *Reule*.

Reyse, to make an inroad or military expedition.

Reyn, reyne, sb. rain, vb. to rain, 617.

Rially, riallyche, royally.

Richesse, riches, 397. This word, as well as *alms*, is a singular noun derived immediately from the French.

Riden, to ride.

Rightes, rightly, 994. *At alle rightes* = rightly in all respects.

Rome, to walk, roam, 207.

Ronne, ronnen, pret. pl. *ran*, 2067.

Rood, rode.

Roos, rose.

Roost, a roast.

Roote, rote. *By roote* = by rote.

Rore, to roar, 2023. A.S. *raran*.

Roste, to roast.

Rote, a harp. See *Roote*.

Roughte, cared for. See *Recche*.

Rouke, to lie close, cower down, to *ruck*, 450.

Rouncy, a hackney. Fr. *roncin*.

Roundel, song, 671.

Route, rowte, a company, assembly.

Routhe, rowthe, pity, compassion, sorrow, 56. See *Rewe*.

Rudelyche, rudely.

Ruggy, rugged, rough (lit. torn, broken, uneven), 2025.

Ryal, royal, 639.

Ryally, royally, 829.

Ryngen, ring, resound, 1742.

Ryt, rides, 126.

Sad, sober, staid, 2127.

Sadly, firmly, 1744.

Salue, to salute, 634.

Saluyng, salutation, 791.

Sangwin, of a blood-red color.

Sauce, saucer.

Sauf, save, except.

Saufly, safely.

Saugh, sawgh, sauh (pret. of *se*), saw.

Save, the herb sage or *salvia*, 1855.

Sawce, sauce; from Lat. *sal*, salt.

Sawceflem, pimpled.

Sawe, a saying, word, discourse, 668.

Sawtrie, a psaltery, a musical instrument something like a harp.

Say (pret. of *se*), saw.

Sayn, to say.

Scape, to escape, 249.

Scarsly, parsimoniously.

Schaft, an arrow, shaft, 504.

Schake, p.p. shaken.

Schamefast, modest, 1197. *Schamfastnesse*, modesty.

Schap, form, shape, 1031.

Schape, schapen, p.p. destined, planned, 534.

Schape, schapen, to plan, purpose, ordain, 250.

Schaply, fit, likely.

Schave, shaven.

Sche, she.

Scheeld, scheld, a shield, 1264.

Scheeldes, coins called crowns.

Scheene, schene, bright, fair, beautiful, 210.

Schent, p.p. *schende*, hurt destroyed, 1896.

Schepne, stables, 1142.

Schere, shears, 1559. To this root belong *shear*, *share*, *shire*, *shore*, *plough-share*, a *sheard*, or *sherd* (as in *pot-sherd*), *short*, *skirt*, *shirt*.

Scherte, a shirt.

Schet, p.p. shut, 1739. It is connected with *shoot*; for to *shut* is to close the door by means of a *bolt* or *bar* driven forwards.

Schipman, a sailor.

Schires ende = end of a *shire* or county.

Schirreve, the governor (reeve) of a shire or county. See *Reeve*.

Schode, the temple (of the head), properly the parting of the hair of a man's head, *not*, as Tyrwhitt and others say, the hair itself, 1149.

Scholde, schulde, should.

Schon, shone.

Schoo, a shoe.

Schorte, to shorten. See *Shere*.

Schorteliche, briefly, 627.

Schowte, to shout.

Schrewe, to curse, beshrew: hence *shrewd*. Originally O.E. *shrewed* = wicked, and hence crafty, sharp, intelligent, clearsighted.

Schrighte, schrykede, shrieked, 1959.

Schul, pl. shall, 889.

Schuld, schulde, should.

Schulder, a shoulder. *Schuldered*, shouldered, having shoulders. A.S. *scylan*, to divide; whence *scale*, *skill*, *scull*, *shell*, *shield*, *shale*, *sill*.

Schuln, pl. shall, 498.

Schynes, shins, legs, 421.

Schyvere, to shatter, 1747.

Sclender, slender. It is probably only a sibilant form of *lean*.

Scole, a school. *Scoler*, a scholar.

Scoleye, to attend school, to study.

Seche, seke, to seek, as in be-*seech*.

Secre, secret.

Seek, seeke, sick. *Seeknesse*, sickness, 39S.

Seene, to see, 56.

Seet (pl. *seeten*), sat, 1217, 2035.

Sege, a siege, 79.

Seide (pret. of *seye*), said.

Seie, seye, to say.

Seigh (pret. of *se*), saw.

Seint, seinte, saint.

Seistow, sayest thou, 267.

Seith, saith, says.

Seke, to seek. See *Seche*.

Seke, pl. sick. See *Seek*.

Seknesse, sickness, 453.

Selde, seldom, 681.

Selle, give, sell.

Selle, house, cell.

Selve, same, 1726. Cp. "the *self-same* day," etc. A.S. *seolf*. Ger. *selbst*.

Sely, simple, happy.

Seme (vb. impers.), to seem.

Semely, seemly, comely, elegant, what is beseeming. O.E. *seme*, seemly.

Semycope, a short cope.

Sen, seen, seene, sene, to see. to be seen, 415, 499.

Sendal, a thin silk.

Sentence, sense, meaning, judgment, matter of a story.

Sergeant (or Sergeaunt) of law, a servant of the sovereign for his law business.

Sermonyng, preaching, 2233.

Servage, bondage, 1088.

Servaunt, a servant, 1377.

Servysable, willing to be of service.

Serye, series, 2209.

Sesoun, season.

Seten (p.p. of *sette*), sat, 594.

Sethe, to boil, seethe.

Seththen, since. See *Sith*.

Seurte, security, surety, 746.

Sewed, followed.

Sey, saw. See *Seigh*.

Sey, seye, seyn, to say (pret. *seyde*).

Seyh, saw. See *Seigh*.

Seyl, a sail.

Seyn, p.p. seen.

Seynd (p.p. of *senge*), singed, toasted.

Seynt, seynte, holy, a saint, 863.

Seynt, a girdle.

Shef, a sheaf.

Shorteliche, shortly, briefly, 627.

Sight, providence, 814.

Sik (pl. *sike*), sick, 742. See *Seek*.

Sike, a sigh; vb. to sigh. See *Swough*.

Siker, syker, sure, certain, 2191.

Sikerly, surely, certainly, truly.

Sistren, sisters, 161.

Sit, sits, 740.

Sith, sithe, sithes, time, times, 1019.

Sith, siththen, since, afterwards, 72, 431, 545, 663, 1244.

kalled, having the *scall*, *scale*, or *scab*, scurfy.

Skape, to escape. See *Scape*.

Skathe, loss, misfortune. It still exists in *scatheless*, *scathing*.

Sklendre, slender.

Slake, slow, 2043. See *Aslake.*

Slaughtre, a slaughter, 1173.

Slawe (p.p. of *sle*), slain.

Slee, sleen, slen, to slay, 364.

Sleep (pret. of *slepe*), slept.

Sleere, a slayer, 1147.

Sleeth, slays, 260.

Sleighly, prudently, wisely, 586. It is not used in a bad sense.

Sleighte, contrivance, craft.

Slep, slept. See *Sleep.*

Slepen, to sleep.

Slepy, causing sleep, 529.

Slepyng, sleep.

Sleves, sleeves.

Slider, slippery, 406. With the root *slide* are connected *sledge* (O.E. *sled*), *slade*, etc.

Sloggardye, sloth, 184. O.E. *slogge*, to be sluggish; whence *slug, sluggish.*

Slough, slowh (pret. of *sle*), slew, 122, 1608.

Smal, smale, small.

Smerte, adj. smarting, sharp, grievous; adv. sharply, smartly.

Smerte (pret. *smerte*), to pain, hurt, displease, 536.

Smokyng, perfuming, 1423.

Smoot, smot (pret. of *smite*). smote, 846.

Smothe, smooth, smoothly.

Snewede, *snowed,* swarmed, abounded.

Snybbe, to reprove, snub.

Soberly, sad, solemn.

Socour, succor, 60.

Sodein, sodeyn, sudden. *Sodeinly, Sodeynliche, Sodeynly,* suddenly, 260, 717.

Solaas, solas, solace, mirth.

Solempne, festive, important.

Solempnely, pompously.

Solempnite, feast, festivity, 12.

Som, some, 397, 399. Cp. *som . . . som* = one . . . other.

Somdel, somewhat.

Somer, summer.

Sompnour, an officer employed to summon delinquents to appear in ecclesiastical courts, now called an apparitor.

Sond, sand.

Sondry, sundry, various.

Sone, soon, 562.

Sone, a son.

Song, pret. sang, 197. *Songe,* p.p. sung.

Sonne, the sun, 5.

Soo, so.

Sop (in wyn).

Soper, supper.

Sore, soor, sb. grief, 1836; adv. sorely, 536.

Sort, destiny, chance.

Sorwe, sb. sorrow, 361, 419. *Sorwen,* vb. to be sorrowful, grieve.

Sorweful, sorrowful, 212.

Sory, sorrowful, 1146, 1152. "*Sory* comfort" = discomfort; "*sory* grace" = misfortune.

Soth, sooth, sothe, sb. truth; adj. true, 768. It still exists in *forsooth, soothsayer.*

Sothely, sothly, truly.

Sothfastnesse, truth.

Sotil, sotyl, subtle, fine-wrought, 196, 1172.

Soun, sown, a sound, to sound.

Souper, supper.

Souple, supple, pliant.

Soveraignly, surpassingly.

Sovereyn, high, supreme, sovereign.

Sowle, soul, 1005.

Sowne, vb. to sound; sb. sound.

Sownynge in, tending to.

Spak, spake.

Spare, to refrain, abstain from.

Sparre, bar, bolt (Eng. *spar*), 132.

Sparthe, a battle-axe, or halberd, 1662.

Sparwe, a sparrow.

Special, "in special," specially.

Speede, to speed, succeed (pret. *spedde*), 359.

Speken, to speak (pret. *spak*).

Spere, a spear, 781.

Spiced, sophisticated, or scrupulous.

Spicerie, spices, 2077. *spices =* species, kinds.

Spores, spurs. A.S. *spura*, *spora*, Ger. *Sporn ;* whence Eng. *spurn*.

Sprad, p.p. spread, 2045.

Springen, to spring, 1749. A.S. *sprengan ;* Sw. *springa*, *spricka*, to burst, spring; Ger. *sprengen*, to scatter, burst open ; Eng. *sprig*, *spray*, *sprinkle*, *spruce*, belong to this family of words.

Spronge (p.p. of *springe*), sprung, 579.

Squyer, a squire.

Stabled, established, 2137.

Stalke, to step slowly and stealthily, 621.

Starf (pret. of *sterve*), died, 75. See *Sterve*.

Steep, stepe, bright, glittering; not deep or sunken, as it is generally explained.

Steer, a yearling bullock, a *steer* or stirk, 1291.

Stele, to steal (pret. *stal*, p.p. *stole*, *stolen*).

Stemede, shone. O.E. *stem*, *steem*, a gleam of light.

Stenten (pret. *stente*, p.p. *stent*), to stop, cease, 45, 510. A.S. *stintan*, to be blunt; *stunt*, blunt, blockish.

Sterre, a star.

Stert, 847. *At a stert =* in a moment, immediately.

Sterte, to start, leap, escape (pret. *sterte*, p.p. *stert*), 186, 222, 644.

Sterve, to die, 286.

Steven, stevene, (1) voice,

sound, 1704; (2) a time appointed by previous agreement, 666.

Stewe, a fish-pond.

Stille, quietly, secretly, 145.

Stith, an anvil, 1168.

Stiward, a steward. A.S. *stiward*, a steward; O.N. *stivardr*, the person whose business it is to look to the daily work of an establishment; *stjá*, domestic occupation; Norse *stia*, to be busy about the house; O.N. *stia*, a sheep-house (Eng. *sty*). The syllable -*ward =* keeper.

Stoke = *steke*, to stick, 1688.

Stole, p.p. stolen, 1769.

Stomble, to stumble, 1755. O.E. *stumpe*, O.N. *stumpa*, to totter, fall. It is connected with *stam-mer*, *stump*, *stub*.

Stonde, stonden, to stand (pret. *stod*, p.p. *stonde*, *stonden*).

Stonge, stongen, p.p. stung, 221.

Stoon, stone. A.S. *stán*.

Stoor, store, stock (of a farm). O.Fr. *estôr*, Mid. Lat. *staurum*, store. O.Fr. *estorer*, to erect, build, garnish (Lat. *instaurere*). *Telle no store =* set no value upon, set no store by.

Stope (p.p. of *steppe*, to step), advanced. A.S. *steppan* (pret. *stop*, p.p. *ge-stopen*), to step, advance.

Stot, a stallion, a *stoat* (which also signifies a weasel). A.S. *stotte*, a horse, hack; *stod* (in composition), a stallion ; Du. *stuyte*. The Promptorium Parvulorum has "*stot*, a horse, cabalus."

Stounde, a moment, a short space of time, 354. A.S. *stund*, a short space, space of time; O.H. Ger. *stunt*, a moment; Ger. *Stunde*, an hour.

Stoute, stowte, strong, brave, 1296.

Straughte (pret. of *strecche*), stretched, 2058.

Straunge, foreign. O.Fr. *estrange*, Lat. *extraneus*, from *extra*, without.

Stre, stree, straw, 2060. A.S. *streow*, Norse *strá*; A.S. *streowian*, Ger. *streuen*, to strew.

Strecche, to stretch. O.E. *streke*, to stretch; A.S. *streccan*, to stretch; *strec*, rigid, violent; with which are connected *streak*, *strike*, *stroke*, *stark*, &c.

Streem, stream, river.

Streepe, to strip, 148. We have the other form of this root in *strip*, *stripe*, *strap*.

Streite, drawn.

Streyne, to constrain.

Streyt, close, narrow, stinted. *strict*.

Streyte, closely. O.Fr. *estroit*, It. *stretto*, strait, narrow; Lat. *stringere*, *strictum*, to strain.

Strif, stryf, strife, contest, 1580. O.Fr. *estrif*, strife; *estriver*, Ger. *streben*, to strive.

Strike (of flax), a hank.

Strof (pret. of *strive*), strove, disputed, vied with, 180.

Strond, stronde, strand.

Strook, a stroke, 843.

Stubbes, stumps, trunks, 1120. A.S. *styb*, Du. *stobbe*, stump; whence, *stubborn*, *stubble*.

Stynt, imp. sing. stop, 1490.

Stynte, stynten, to stop (pret. *stynte*), 1513. See *Stenten*.

Subtilly, craftily.

Suffisaunce, sufficiency.

Suffisaunt, sufficient, 773.

Sunge, sungen, p.p. sung.

Surcote, an upper coat.

Susteene, to sustain, 1135.

Suster (pl. *sustres*), a sister, 13.

Swelte, fainted, 498. A.S. *sweltan*, to die, perish (through heat).

Swerd, a sword.

Swere, to swear, 963. We have the same root in an-*swer*.

Swet, swete, sweet.

Sweven, a dream. O.N. *sofa*, to sleep.

Swich, such; *swich sorwe*, so great sorrow, 4.

Swinke, swynke, to labor, toil.

Swinkere, a laborer.

Swoot, swoote, swote, sweet, 1569.

Swor, swore. See *Swere*.

Swough, the raging of the elements, a storm, 1121.

Swowne, to swoon, 55, 1961. The O.E. *swoghe* shows that *swoon* is connected with *sigh*, *sough*, &c.

Swymbel, a moaning, sighing sort of noise, caused by the wind, 1121.

Swyn (sing. and pl.), swine.

Swynk, sb. labor, toil.

Syk, syke, sick.

Syke, sb. a sigh, 1062; vb. to sigh, 2127. See *Sike*.

Syn, since. See *Sith*.

Sythens, since. See *Sith*.

Taas, tas, heap, 147, 151, 162.

Tabard, the sleeveless coat on which arms were embroidered; a herald's coat of arms. It was the old dress of the laborer, and Chaucer applies it to the loose frock of the ploughman.

Taffata, taffeta.

Taille, a tally, an account scored in a notched piece of wood.

Tak, imper. take, 226.

Take, p.p. taken, 1789.

Takel, an arrow. It seems to have signified any sort of implement or utensil, whether used as a tool or weapon.

Tale, speech, discourse. *Telle tale* = take account of, estimate.

Talen, to tell tales.

Tallege = to allege, 2142.

Tapicer, an upholsterer. Fr. *tapis,* a carpet.

Tappestere, a female tapster.

Targe, a target or shield. Fr. *targe.*

Tathenes = to Athens, 165.

Techen, to teach.

Teene, vexation, annoyance, 2247.

Tendite, to endite, tell, 351.

Teres. tears, 422.

Tespye, to espy.

Testers, head-pieces or hemlets, 1641.

Thabsence, the absence, 381.

Thankes, thonkes, the genitive of *thank,* 768. 1249. Used adverbially with the personal pronouns (possessive), *his thankes,* he being willing.

Thanne, then.

Tharmes, the arms, 2058.

Tharray, the array.

Thavys, the advice, 2218.

The, to thrive, prosper.

Theffect. the effect, 331.

Thei, they. The Northern form is *tha* or *thai;* the Southern *heo, hi.*

Thencens, thensens, the incense, 1419.

Thenchauntementz, the enchantments, 1086.

Thencres, the increase.

Thenke, (1) to think; (2) to seem. *Thank* is another form of the root. See *Thinke.*

Thentre, the entrance, 1125.

Ther, there, where.

Therto, besides.

Thes, these, 673.

Thestat, the state or rank.

Thider, thither, 405.

Thilke, the like, that, 335, 1525.

Thinke, thynke, to seem. It is used impersonally, as "me *thinketh*" = it seems to me.

Thirle, to pierce, 1852. A S. whence *nostrils* (O.E. *nosethirles*), *thrill, trill.*

Thise, pl. these.

Tho, pl. the, those, 265, 1493.

Tho, then, 135.

Thoffice, the office, 2005.

Thombe, thumb.

Thonder, thunder. A.S. *thunor,* Ger. *Donner.* With this class of words are connected *din, dun, stun.*

Thonke, thank.

Thorisoun, the orison or prayer, 1403.

Thral, slave, serf, one enslaved, 694.

Thred, threed, thread, 1172; *Thredbare,* threadbare.

Thresshe, to thrash.

Threste, to thrust, press, 1754.

Thridde, third, 605.

Thries, thrice.

Thurgh, through, 362.

Thurgh-fare, a *thorough* fare, 1989. Cp. Goth. *thairh,* Ger. *durch,* Eng. *through* and *thorough.*

Thurgh-girt. See *Girt.*

Til, to, 620.

To, at.

To-breste, burst asunder, 1753. See *Breste.*

To-brosten, burst or broken in pieces, 1833, 1899.

To-hewen, hewed or cut in pieces, 1751.

Tollen, to take toll or payment. A.S. *tól,* tax. The Romance form of the root is seen in *tally, tailor, entail, retail, tallage.*

To-morn, to-morrow. See *Morwe.* The *to* (as in *to-yere* = this year) is the prep. *to,* as in O.E. *togedere,* together.

Ton, toes.

Tonge, tongue.

Tonne-greet, having the circumference as great as a tun, 1130.

Too, toe, 1868.

Tool, weapon.

Toon, toes.

Top, head.

Toret, turret, 1051.

Torettz, rings, 1294.

Torne, to turn, 630. Fr. *tourner*. The root *tor*, turn, twist, is seen in the Lat. *tornus*, a lathe; *torquere*, to twist; *turben*, a whirlwind.

To-schrede, cut in shreds, 1751. See *Schere*.

Toun, town.

Tour, tower, 172, 419.

Trace, track, path.

Trapped, having trappings, 2032.

Trappures, trappings of a horse, 1641.

Traunce, a trance, 714.

Trays, the traces by which horses draw, horse-harness, 1281.

Treccherie, treachery.

Trede, to tread, 2164.

Tresoun, treason, 1143.

Trespace, trespass, 960.

Tresse, a tress, plait, 191.

Treté, treaty, 430.

Tretys, long and well-proportioned.

Trewe, true. *Trewely*, truly.

Trompe, trumpe, a trumpet, a trumpeter, 1316.

Tronchoun, a headless spear or truncheon, 1757.

Trouthe, truth, troth, 752.

Trowe, to believe. *Trow* = I think it to be true.

Trussed up, packed up.

Tukked, tucked, coated.

Tunge, a tonge.

Tuo, two.

Turneying, turneynge, a tourment, 1699. See *Torne*.

Tway, twayn, twayne, twey, tweye, twoo, tuo, two, twain, 40, 270. With this root we must connect *twin*, *twine*, *twill*, *twig*. It appears also in *twelve* ($= 2 + 10$), and *twenty* (2×10).

Twynne, to depart, separate. See *Tway*.

Tyde, time. A.S. *tid*, time; whence *tidy*, *tides*.

Typet, tippet.

Typtoon, tiptoes. See *Toon*.

Unce, a small portion. (Eng. *ounce*.)

Uncouth, uncouthe. uncowth, unkouthe, unknown, rare, *uncouth*, 1639. See *Couthe*.

Undergrowe, undergrown.

Undern, the time of the mid-day meal. A.S. *undern*, the third hour of the day. It signifies literally the intervening period, and hence a part of the forenoon, a meal taken at that time.

Undertake, to affirm.

Unknowe, unknown, 548.

Unkonnyng, unknowing, not *cunning* (knowing), ignorant. In our English Bible the word *cunning* is used in a good sense, 1538.

Unset, not at a set time, not appointed, 666.

Unwist, unknown, 2119. See *Wite*.

Unyolden, not having yielded, 1784. See *Yolden*.

Uphaf (pret. of *upheve*), upheaved, uplifted, 1570. See *Heve*.

Upright, flat on the back, 1150.

Upriste, uprising, 193.

Up-so-down, upside down, 519.

Upstert, upsterte, upstarted, arose, 441. See *Sterte*.

Upyaf, gave up, 1569.

Vasselage, valor, courage (displayed in the service rendered by a *vassal)*, 2196.

Vavasour. A *Vavasour* was most probably a sub-vassal holding a small fief, a sort of esquire.

Venerye, hunting, 1450. Lat. *venari*, to hunt, chase; whence *venison*.

Ventusyng, cupping, a surgical term, 1889.

Venym, poison, venom, 1893.

Verdite, verdict, judgment, sentence.

Verray, verrey, true, very. *Verraily*, truly.

Vese, a rush of wind, draught, gush; lit. an impulse, 1127. Lat. *impetus.* Hence probably the modern Eng. *fuss.* (Skeat.)

Vestimenz, vestments, 2090.]

Veyn, vain, 236.

Veyne blood, blood of the veins, 1889.

Viage, voyage.

Vigilies, vigils.

Vileinye, sb. unbecoming conduct, disgrace, 84.

Vitaille, victuals.

Vouchesauf, to vouchsafe, grant.

Voyde, to expel, 1893.

Waar, aware, wary. See *War.*

Wake-pleyes, ceremonies attending the vigils for the dead, 2102.

Walet, a wallet.

Wan, won, conquered, 131. See *Winne.*

Wane, to decrease, diminish, 1220.

Wanhope, despair, 391. See *Wane.*

Wantown, wanton, free, unrestrained. The prefix *wan =* *-un; -town = -togen*, trained.

Wantownesse, wantonness.

War, aware, cautious, prudent. A.S. *wær, war*, caution. "I was *waar*."

Ware, to warn, to cause one to beware.

Wastel-breed, bread-cake. O. Fr. *gasteau*, a cake.

Waterles, without water.

Wawes, waves, 1100.

Wayke, weak, 29.

Wayleway, welaway, alas ! well-a-way ! well-a-day ! 80.

Waymentyng, weymentyng, a lamentation, wailing, 137, 1063.

Wayte, to be on the look out for, to look for, 364. See *Awayt.*

Webbe, a weaver.

Wedde, pledge, security, 360. "*to wedde*" = for a pledge.

Wedden, to wed, 974.

Wede, clothing, 148. It is still retained in "widow's *weeds.*"

Weel, well, 68, 1265.

Wel, adv. full, very, 653; much, 396.

Wele, weal, prosperity, wealth, 37.

Welle, source, fountain, 2179.

Wende, weened, thought, 411.

Wende, wenden, to go, pass away, 1356. The Eng. *went* is the past tense of *wende.* Cp. the phrase "to *wend* one's way."

Wene, to ween, think, 797. It is preserved in E. *ween, over-weening*, &c.

Wenged, winged, 527.

Wep, weep, wept, 1487. Cp. O.E. *crep, lep* = crept, leapt.

Wepe, wepen (pret. *weep, wep;* p.p. *wepen*), to weep.

Wepen, wepne, a weapon, 733.

Werche, wirche, werken, to work, 1901.

Were, to defend, guard, 1692.

We rede, wore.

Werre, war.

Werreye, werreyen, to make war against, 626, 686.

Werse, worse, 366.

Werte, a wart.

Wessch (pret. of *wasche*), washed, 1425.

Wete, wet, moist, 422.

Wette, wetted.

Wex, sb. wax.

Wexe, to increase, grow, become. A.S. *weaxan*, to increase. *Wex*, increased, became, 504. Shakespeare has "a man of *wax*" = an adult, a man of full growth.

Wexyng, growing, increasing, 1220.

Wey, weye, a way.

Weyeth, weigheth, esteems, 923.

Weyle, to wail; to cry *wei!* or *woe!* 363.

Weymentynge, 44. See *Waymentyng*.

Whan, whanne, when.

What, lo! wherefore, why.

Whel, wheel, 1165.

Whelkes, pimples, blotches, Ger. *welken*, to wither, fade, dry.

Wher, where, 1952.

Wher, whether, 1394.

Whether, whether, which of two, 998.

Which, what. *Which a* = what a, 1817.

Whil, whilst. *While*, time. A.S. *hwile*, time; Norse *hvíla*, to rest. It is retained in *awhile;* "to *while* away the time" = to pass the time away in rest or recreation. *Whiles*, whilst.

Whilom, formerly, once. 1, 1545. The *-um* was an old adverbial ending, as seen in O.E. *ferrum*, afar. Eng. *seldom*.

Whit, white. Comp. *whitter*,

Whyppyltre, the cornel-tree, 2065.

Widewe, wydwe, a widow.

Wif, wyf, wife, woman.

Wight, any living creature; a person male or female.

Wight, wighte, weight, 1287.

Wikke, wicked, bad, untoward, 229. O.E. *wikke*, poor, mean, *weak*.

Wilfully, willingly.

Wilne, to desire, 751.

Wiltou, wilt thou, 686.

Wilwe, willow-tree, 2064.

Winne, wynne (pret. *wan, won;* p.p. *wonne, wonnen*), to win, obtain, gain, 759.

Wirche, to work, 1901.

Wis, wys, wise.

Wis = *iwis*, certainly, 1928. "As *wis* = as certainly, as truly. See *Iwis*.

Wise, wyse, mode, manner, 481, 882. See *Gyse*.

Wisly, wysly, truly, 1376. See *Iwis*.

Wit, understanding, judgment, wisdom, 279, 746.

Wite, wyte, to know, to learn, 402, 977; 1st and 3d pers. sing. indic. *wot, woot;* 2d pers. *wost;* pl. *witen, wyten;* pret. *wiste*. A.S. *witan*, to know; whence *wit, to wit, witty,* &c.

Withholde, maintained.

Withouten, without, besides.

Withsayn, withseie, to gainsay, 282.

Wityng, knowledge, 753. See *Wite*.

Wive, wyve, dat. of *wif, wyf*.

Wlatsome, loathsome, hateful, 233.

Wo, woo, sb. sorrow, woe: adj. sorrowful, grieved, displeased.

Wode. See *Wood*.

Wodly, madly, 443. See *Wood*.

Wofullere, the more sorrowful, 482.

Wol, wole, vb. will, pl. *wolden.*

Wolde, would.

Wolle (pl. of *wole*), will.

Woln (pl.), will, 1263.

Wolt, wilt; *Woltow,* wilt thou, 299.

Wommanhede, womanly feeling, 890.

Wonder, wonderfully, 796.

Wonder, wonderful, 1215.

Wonderly, wonderfully.

Wone, custom, usage, 182.

Wone, to dwell, 2069.

Wonne, wonnen (p.p. of *winne*), conquered, obtained, 19.

Wonyng, a dwelling, habitation.

Woo, sorrowful lament, 42.

Wood, wode, mad, 471. A.S. *wód,* mad; *wódnes,* madness.

Woodebynde, a woodbine, 650.

Woodnesse, madness, 1153.

Wook, awoke, 535.

Woot (1st pers.), know. See *Wite.*

Worschipe, to honor, to pay proper respect to another's *worth,* 1393.

Worschipe, sb. honor; *Worschipful,* honorable, 1054.

Wortes, herbs. A.S. *weort, wyrt.* It still exists in *colewort, orchard* (= *wort-yard,* herb-garden).

Worthi, worthy, brave. *Worthinesse,* bravery.

Wost, knowest, 305. *Wot, Woot,* knows, 28. See *Wite.*

Wrastle, to wrestle, 2103.

Wrastlynge, wrestling.

Wrecche, a wretch, wretched, 63, 73, 248.

Wreke, to revenge, avenge, wreak, 103.

Wrethe, a wreath, a derivative from the vb. to *writhe,* 1287.

Wrighte, a carpenter (literally, a workman). Cp. *wheelwright, playwright.*

Writ, wrote.

Wroth, angry.

Wyd, wide.

Wyf. See *Wif.*

Wyke, a week, 681.

Wympel, a covering for the neck. *Ywympled,* decked with a *wymple.* Fr. *guimple.*

Wyn, wine.

Wynnynge, gain, profit.

Wys, wise. *Wysly,* wisely.

Wyte, wyten, know. See *Wite.*

Yaf (pret. of *yeve* or *yive*), gave.

Yate, a gate, 557. This old pronunciation still survives in some parts of England.

Ybete, beaten, 1304.

Ybrent, burnt, 88.

Ybrought, brought, 253.

Yburied, buried, 88.

Ycleped, yclept, called. See *Clepe.*

Ycome, come.

Ycorve, cut, 1155.

Ydon, done.

Ydrawe, drawn, 86.

Ydropped, bedropped, covered with drops, 2026.

Ydryve, ydriven, driven, 1149.

Ye, yea, the answer to a question asked in the affirmative form, 809; *yis, yes,* being the affirmative answer to a question asked in the negative form.

Yeddynges, songs; properly the gleeman's songs.

Yeeldyng, yielding, return, produce.

Yeer, yer, year, 523.

Yeldehalle = *geldehall,* a guildhall.

Yelle, to yell; *Yelleden* (pl. pret.), yelled.

Yelpe, to boast, 1380. (Eng. *yelp.*)

Yelwe, yellow, 191, 1071. It is connected with *gold, gall, yolk,* &c.

Yeman, a yeoman, commoner, a feudal retainer. Tyrwhitt refers it to *yeongeman,* a young man, a vassal.

Yer, yeer, a year (pl. *yeer,* years).

Yerd, yerde, rod, 529; as in *yard*-measure.

Yerd, enclosure, yard. A.S. *geard,* hedge, enclosure, garden; Eng. *yard, orchard, garden.*

Yeve, yeven, yive, to give, 223.

Yeve, yeven, p.p. given, 57.

Yfounde, found, 353.

Ygrounde, p.p. ground, sharpened, 1691.

Yholde, p.p. esteemed, held, 1516, 2100.

Yifte, gift, 1340.

Yit, yet. *Yit now* = just now, 298.

Yive, yiven, to give.

Ylik, alike, 1876.

Ymaginyng, plotting, 1137.

Ymaked, p p. made, 1997.

Ymet, p.p. met, 1766.

Yymeynd (p.p. of *menge*), mingled, mixed, 1312. A.S. *mengian,* to mix.

Ynned, lodged, entertained, 1334.

Ynough, ynowgh, enough. See *Inough.*

Yolden, p.p. yielded, repaid, 2194.

Yolle, to yell, 1814.

Yollyng, yelling, 420.

Yond, yonder, 241.

Yong, yonge, young.

Yore, of a long time. *Yore ago* = a long time ago, 955; *of yore,* in olden time. A.S. *geara,* of yore, from *gear,* a year.

Yow, you.

Ypayed, payed, 944.

Yraft, bereft, 1157.

Yronnen, p.p. run, coagulated, 1835.

Ysene, to be seen.

Yserved, p.p. served, 105.

Yslayn, slain, 1850.

Yspreynd (p.p. of *sprenge*), sprinkled, scattered, 1311.

Ystert, p.p. started, escaped, 734.

Ystorve, dead, 1156.

Yteyd, tied.

Ytorned, p.p. turned, 380.

Yturned, turned, 1204.

Ywis, ywys, certain, sure. See *Iwis.*

Ywont, wont, accustomed. See *Wone.*

Ywrought, worked, wrought.

Ywympled, decked with a wimple. See *Wympel.*

A TEXT-BOOK ON RHETORIC;

SUPPLEMENTING THE DEVELOPMENT OF THE SCIENCE WITH EXHAUSTIVE PRACTICE IN COMPOSITION.

A Course of Practical Lessons Adapted for use in High Schools and Academies, and in the Lower Classes of Colleges.

BY

BRAINERD KELLOGG, A.M.,

Professor of the English Language and Literature in the Brooklyn Collegiate and Polytechnic Institute, and one of the authors of Reed & Kellogg's "Graded Lessons in English" and "Higher Lessons in English."

In preparing this work upon Rhetoric, the author's aim has been to write a practical text-book for High Schools, Academies, and the lower classes of Colleges, based upon the science rather than an exhaustive treatise upon the science itself.

This work has grown up out of the belief that the rhetoric which the pupil needs is not that which lodges finally in the memory, but that which has worked its way down into his tongue and fingers, enabling him to speak and write the better for having studied it. The author believes that the aim of the study should be to put the pupil in possession of an art, and that this can be done not by forcing the science into him through eye and ear, but by drawing it out of him, in products, through tongue and pen. Hence all explanations of principles are followed by exhaustive practice in Composition—to this everything is made tributary.

"KELLOGG's RHETORIC is evidently the fruit of scholarship and large experience. The author has collected his own materials, and disposed of them with the skill of a master; his statements are precise, lucid, and sufficiently copious. Nothing is sacrificed to show; the book is intended for use, and the abundance of examples in the eyes of the thorough teacher."—*Prof. A. S. Cook. Johns Hopkins University, Baltimore, Md.*

"This is just the work to take the place of the much-stilted 'Sentential Analysis' that is being waded through to little purpose by the Grammar and High School pupils of our country. This work not only teaches the discipline of analyzing thought, but leads the student to feel that it is *his* thought that is being dealt with, dissected, and unfolded, to efficient expression."—*Prof. G. S. Albee, Prest. of State Normal School, Oshkosh, Wis.*

276 pages, 12mo, attractively bound in cloth.

CLARK & MAYNARD, Publishers, New York.

ENGLISH CLASSIC SERIES,

FOR

Classes in English Literature, Reading, Grammar, e

EDITED BY EMINENT ENGLISH AND AMERICAN SCHOLARS.

Each Volume contains a Sketch of the Author's Life, Prefatory and Explanatory Notes, etc., etc.

1 Byron's Prophecy of Dante. (Cantos I. and II.)
2 Milton's L'Allegro and Il Penseroso.
3 Lord Bacon's Essays, Civil and Moral. (Selected.)
4 Byron's Prisoner of Chillon.
5 Moore's Fire-Worshipers. (Lalla Rookh. Selected from Parts I. and II.)
6 Goldsmith's Deserted Village.
7 Scott's Marmion. (Selections from Canto VI.)
8 Scott's Lay of the Last Minstrel. (Introduction and Canto I.)
9 Burns' Cotter's Saturday Night, and Other Poems.
10 Crabbe's The Village.
11 Campbell's Pleasures of Hope. (Abridgment of Part I.)
12 Macaulay's Essays on Bunyan's Pilgrim's Progress.
13 Macaulay's Armada, and other Poems.
14 Shakespeare's Merchant of Venice. (Selections from Acts I., III. and IV.)
15 Goldsmith's Traveler.
16 Hogg's Queen's Wake.
17 Coleridge's Ancient Mariner.
18 Addison's Sir Roger de Coverley.
19 Gray's Elegy in a Country Churchyard.
20 Scott's Lady of the Lake. (Canto I.)
21 Shakespeare's As You Like It, etc. (Selections.)
22 Shakespeare's King John and King Richard II. (Selections.)
23 Shakespeare's King Henry IV., King Henry V., King Henry VI. (Selections.)
24 Shakespeare's Henry VIII. and Julius Cæsar. (Selections.)
25 Wordsworth's Excursion. (Book I.)
26 Pope's Essay on Criticism.
27 Spenser's Faerie Queene. (Cantos I. and II.)
28 Cowper's Task. (Book I.)
29 Milton's Comus.
30 Tennyson's Enoch Arden.
31 Irving's Sketch Book. (Selectio
32 Dickens' Christmas Carol. (Condens
33 Carlyle's Hero as a Prophet
34 Macaulay's Warren Hasting (Condens
35 Goldsmith's Vicar of Wakefi (Condens
36 Tennyson's The Two Voices a A Dream of Fair Women.
37 Memory Quotations. For us High Schools and upper cla of Grammar Schools.
38 Cavalier Poets.
39 Dryden's Alexander's Feast a MacFleknoe.
40 Keats' The Eve of St. Agnes
41 Irving's Legend of Slee Hollow.
42 Lamb's Tales from Shakespea
43 Le Row's How to Teach Rea ing. The author of this man has had long and successful perience in teaching this subj
44 Webster's Bunker Hill Oratio
45 The Academy Orthoëpist. Manual of Pronunciation use in the School-room, inclu ing a special list of proper nan of frequent occurrence in lite ture, science and art.
46 Milton's Lycidas, and Hymn the Nativity.
47 Bryant's Thanatopsis, and oth Poems.
48 Ruskin's Modern Painters. (Selection
49 The Shakespeare Speaker. Selections from Shakespea for declamation.
50 Thackeray's Roundabou Papers.
51 Webster's Oration on Adam and Jefferson.
52 Brown's Rab and His Friends
53 Morris's Life and Death of Jason
54 Burke's Speech on America Taxation.
55 Pope's Rape of the Lock.
56 Tennyson's Elaine.
57 Tennyson's In Memoriam.

From 32 to 64 pages each, 16mo. Others in Preparation. Sent by ma on receipt of 12 Cents

PUBLISHED BY CLARK & MAYNARD, 771 BROADWAY NEW YOR

www.ingramcontent.com/pod-product-compliance
Lightning Source LLC
Chambersburg PA
CBHW020236030726
47497CB00009B/3117